The Butcher
of Penetang

Caitlin Press Inc.
8100 Alderwood Road,
Halfmoon Bay, BC, V0N 1Y1
www.caitlin-press.com

Cover photograph: Vici Johnstone
Edited by Patricia Wolfe and Meg Taylor
Text and cover design by the house
Author photo: Laura Sawchuk
Printed in Canada

Caitlin Press Inc. acknowledges financial support from the Government of Canada through the Book Publishing Industry Development Program and the Canada Council for the Arts, and from the Province of British Columbia through the British Columbia Arts Council and the Book Publisher's Tax Credit.

Canada Council for the Arts   Conseil des Arts du Canada

BRITISH COLUMBIA ARTS COUNCIL

Library and Archives Canada Cataloguing in Publication
Trumpener, Betsy

The butcher of Penetang / Betsy Trumpener.

ISBN 978-1-894759-30-4
    I. Title.

PS8639.R845B88 2008   C813'.6   C2008-905634-5

The Butcher of Penetang

stories

Betsy Trumpener

Caitlin Press

For my family: late spring after such long winter

Contents

Let Not Your Hearts be Troubled

Zap Valley

The winter you licked the frosty fence post to see how cold it tasted, you lost days of things you had to say.

A Slip of the Tongue

A Slip of the Tongue

Winter is the long, unplowed road that shuffles you toward home while the dog's breath and a jittery heater warm the car. The windshield is a blur of stars and night, dark and light, like something from the dream where you've lost half your sight. The tape of Tom Waits is slowing from the cold and the juice in your horn has frozen stiff and a tall moose is ankling through the ice and you swerve and heave down a soft pitch off the road and into the ditch. And there you sit, at an odd angle, with the music still "Waltzing Matilda" and your dog dislodged, warming your ear with her breath.

Outside, the snow is still falling. You're jangled and cold. But before too long, before dawn, two men pull up and jump down from their big truck. Happy, like they've been driving the Beaver Forest Road all week, waiting to be heroes, savouring it in their mouths like cherry Lifesavers.

The one man has a stutter and a winch, and the other uses his heavy boots to gun your car until it belches a blue fire and lurches up out of the ditch. And the man with the stutter puts you in the back of his crew cab and offers you hot coffee from the thermos the wife packed back at Summit Lake. He wraps you in a dirty brown sleeping bag and says: "Moose! Huh." And the man with the heavy boots leads your dog out into the snow to follow the moose tracks and you sip coffee in the back of their truck and watch the snow drift.

And later, when you're in your own car again and ready to drive away, you stop to look back. And through the dog's breath on the rear window, you can see those two big men, still standing out on Beaver Road, catching snowflakes with their tongues.

The Butcher of Penetang

When the butcher of Penetang hangs an Easter ewe by her back legs from a hook in the shop's front window, Gabriel and I are ten miles upstream. We're twisting and grinding through the Gibson River rapids in the north of Ontario without our canoe.

By the time the rocks have split open my knee, Gabe is already in the boil, bobbing like an apple. He's swimming after his guitar, a long-snouted musical fish nosing its way through the waves. Gabe doesn't even turn back to warn me.

The Canadian Shield smashes me until I let go of my paddle, until prayers flow out of my knee, until the river blushes with my blood.

Gabe is shouting, "Grab the canoe! Hang onto the boat!" But when I lie down on the stiff white waves, all I can see is sky.

*

The butcher of Penetang comes to the door of his house with a fork in his hand. He opens the screen door with the pressure of his thigh.

"Sorry to bother you," Gabriel tells him. "But this guy who

found us, he said to…He thought you could help."

In fact, the guy who found us had said, "Butcher's a god-damned draft dodger from way back. Talk about fucked up, leaving home 'cause you won't shed blood and end up here, slicing up our cows. And top it off, the fucker's the only guy in town with first aid."

Under the porch light, the butcher can see that I'm bloody and trussed up, my leg splinted to the fractured neck of Gabe's guitar, trailing musical strings and sinew. He stands there in his doorway and combs at his moustache with his fork. He's old and lanky, with curly black hair on his head and his arms.

"What is it, Daddy?" asks a voice from behind his knees.

The butcher smiles. He says, "It's okay, Monika. We've got a patient. Tell Mammi we're going over to the shop. Tell her we'll finish eating later." He sticks the fork in his back pocket.

The butcher comes outside and slings one of my arms around his waist and we walk with Gabe in a slow three-legged race down his long front lawn to the main street. The butcher's body is very warm and he smells slightly of braised beef.

He asks me, "Is it bad? Are you hanging on by just a thread?" He says it so sweetly that I start to cry. He stops to pat me on the back.

"We really appreciate your help and everything," Gabe says, stepping in. "But there's not even a nurse left in town? Or an ambulance?"

He shakes his head. "Nah. Sorry, I'm all you've got."

*

The butcher turns on the fluorescent lights in the butcher shop. I look up at the lamb hanging upside down in the window.

Her wool is half-on and half-off, as if a man had pulled down her pants and then changed his mind.

The butcher lays me down gently on one of the stainless steel counters, and I start to shiver. Monika comes with a pillow under her arms and fluffs it up beneath my head. It smells salty, like tears.

Gabe says he can't bear to watch. He whispers into my hair, "You'll be fine, baby," and goes outside to vomit, and he doesn't come back.

The butcher feeds me shots of Jägermeister and little bites of pepperoni. "Try to relax," he says. "You'll have to trust me." I want to, but I can't stop shaking. Monika holds my leg down, her tiny hands curling around my ankle.

"Sometimes?" Monika says to me. "If my dad is doing, like, a big order, for a freezer or something, I'll sing to him. Sing him songs from camp and stuff." Monika asks if I would like her to sing, if that would help. And she sings me a song about plucking the feathers from a bird, a nice bird. "Alouette, gentille alouette," she sings. "Alouette, je te plumerai."

Her father smiles over at her as he stitches up my leg.

I remember how my father used to sing to me. He used to serenade me with songs from his war, with verses about finger guillotines and whips of hair, singing foreign words that can still make me cry.

And now I lie on that counter in the butcher shop in the village of Penetang and I let the butcher do what he has to do.

I wonder how it would be to have a father like this, to be loved by a man with such gentle, bloody hands.

The Search Party

The girl's uncle cries as he calls out her name. "Hannah! Hannah!" Hannah's mother and her cousins from Prophet River and the forestry crew from the Band Office and the Pine Butte firemen and the Search and Rescue volunteers march shoulder to shoulder to shoulder through the field of wet hay, calling her name. Policemen in orange vests sweep long sticks through the pickled, grey grass defeated by all the rain.

Two white horses watch their slow march across the fields at the edge of town. The animals dip their heads back to the ground hoping for a taste of something. A freight train rushes by, shaking the ground below their feet.

Hannah's mother keeps spotting things in the grass, but when she bends down, there's nothing there but the sharp prick of thistle. She remembers Hannah jogging the Willow Cale Forest Road in her father's old orange hunting vest and new runners, shouting out, "Hey Bear! Hey Bear!" and kicking up gravel dust all the way to the Fraser River and back again. She remembers swimming with her daughter in the hot, shallow pool on Dominion Street and the sweet smell of chlorine left in Hannah's hair.

By the side of the highway, a policewoman reaches her arm around the shoulder of Hannah's oldest cousin. They sit on the bottom step of the Command Post trailer. The cousin tells the policewoman that Hannah once stayed out all night with a sunburned soldier from Cold Lake. The soldier showed up one night at a party at the Tabor Mountain gravel pit. He drove up in a pickup truck with stiff doors and shared his case of beer. He sat by the bonfire with a red, peeling face. He kissed Hannah's ear. He asked her to drive to town with him to get coffee. It was a long way but he called her *Princess*. His truck was all rusty and one of the doors was stuck shut so Hannah had to climb in on his side and crawl over his lap. It was foggy all the way to town, and freezing, and she was shivering. On the drive back, the soldier put his big hand on Hannah's leg and asked her if she'd ever bounced bones. She told him she'd never even tasted coffee.

Hannah made it home the next morning. She was coughing so much she almost threw up. Her mother rushed her to the bathroom sink and tried to steam open her lungs with hot water. She covered Hannah's head with a dark towel and kept her inside the steam. Her mother stroked her back and told Hannah to breathe in and out, in and out. The water in the sink was so hot Hannah had to wipe the steam off the bathroom mirror just to find her own face again.

"The steam?" the policewoman asks. She's distracted by a slash pile of trees and branches burning in the field across the highway. Pale ashes from the fire float up in the wind and twist down on the cars and campers and logging trucks that slow down to watch the search. Travellers roll down their windows. A policeman hands them Xeroxed pictures of Hannah's face. She has short bangs and a big smile. Hannah's neighbours walk the highway shoulder with rakes, scouring the ditches.

The policewoman thinks of her old neighbour back in Sarnia. He asked her to find a ball of dirty socks hidden in his pants. He paid her with a penny and a candy but she ran away and buried them in her backyard. Years later, it still makes her shake. On the Command Post steps, Hannah's oldest cousin starts to sob. She's just remembered something else about the soldier from the gravel pit. He told them he could drink his own urine and never make a face.

Darkness is creeping up on the search party. Hannah's uncle hopes there's still time to call in the tracking dogs. He's willing to walk the pipeline and the Hydro corridor. He knows sweat is enough to kill those caught out in the cold. He prays Hannah is setting signal fires and eating pine cone seeds to keep down her fear. He hopes she's hanging shiny candy wrappers from tree branches, waiting for the first flash of daylight. Hannah's uncle packs up granola bars, a high beam flashlight and a blanket. His pockets are full of little things to outwit the wilds. A bullion cube. Matches dipped in wax. Enough wire to snare a squirrel. Peppermints. He believes hard candy can save a life.

Hannah's uncle walks through the forest, towards the glow of the pulp mill by the river. He calls Hannah's name. He listens as the mill sings some sweet, low tune that never takes a breath.

Have you ever been to the Prince Albert Bus Station?

*E*veryone with broken bones was travelling north with you on the STC bus from Saskatoon. Small boys coming home from hospital, curling the good arm against their mothers. And the men were not drifters. They had babies in their hands. Or they carried long tubes of plans for northern minerals and rocks. Or they were biologists, smelling of deep woods and moss beds. They pencilled little notes in their field books as we rode:

•*Sarsaparilla: woodland herb—historically treated VD*

—now, makes root beer

•*Core Sample Volume values*

•*Today, I felt 100 grams of fear...*

•*To milk a bison, first you must truss it up*

something fierce.

Like this we travelled, with only a short stop in Rosthern. Drove right past the site of the Duck Lake massacre.

In Prince Albert, an old woman was calling to me across

the bus terminal. I could barely see her, waving urgently at me with her body hidden behind the bathroom door.

"Me? Who me?"

I have a thing about bus station bathrooms. I really prefer to use the back of the bus. I don't like to see travellers from Ontario bathing their armpits in the sink. And when you swing open a stall door, you never know what you will find.

This old woman, though, it was nothing like that. She had a broken wrist still swelling in its cast. Arm in a sling on the way to a first cousin's funeral past La Ronge. Five dead this year already, she tells me. Her daughter comes by in the morning to tie up her shoes.

"If you could braid my hair," she says. "Can do nothing for myself now." Not tight, she tells me. Just nice. Her hair is very long and black and thin and I split it in three and then I bring it all back together. I want to say: Thank you for asking.

I light her a smoke, taking the first draw for myself, and pack her fruit from the washroom counter back into her bag. And I find her pain pills.

"Take some, go ahead," she tells me. "It's good for that hard piece of pain."

And then I sit on the dried piss stains on the sidewalk outside the PA bus station and nothing happens. Nothing at all.

Gangster Rap, Ghostkeeper Style

You ate Nechako Nachos and sang karaoke gangster rap at the Ghostkeeper Pub past the edge of Prince George. You rapped a ditty, dirty words and all, no time to take a breath, your heart beating fast from the song's cold little handgun tucked down deep in your big-city pants, damp from a place where sidewalks steam with stink. You rapped that ditty while the waitress with blonde bangs cheered from a high stool at the bar and then got up to sing a Cher song about love. Later, your husband unwrapped his big hands from a round glass of beer and joined her up on stage. And they sang a *Folsom Prison Blues* duet, while your husband tapped his foot on the wooden floor. Your husband was wearing sandals and thick wool socks, the same kind he wore at your wedding. And in the middle of the blues, they jumped up and turned to each other and did a little square dance.

When you drive up the hill to the Ghostkeeper Pub, you can see the river snaking between the pulp mill and the prison. You'll see why you're forbidden to pick up hitchhikers, although it never stops your husband. Since the night he sang those

Folsom Prison Blues, a posse of local prisoners has already made its getaway. There they were in their orange prison jumpsuits, out on a work brigade at the Fall Fair. The prisoners were twirling pink cotton candy, sweet as asbestos, until they jumped into the back of a fast car driven by their sweethearts. They peeled out, wind in their hair, and stripped to their socks as fast as they could.

Soon after, an old convict put on his backpack at dusk at the wilderness prison past Willow River. He climbed on a bicycle. He started pumping those pedals down the service road and was never seen again.

True, a bloodied man carrying an axe once knocked on the door of your next-to-nearest neighbour in the middle of the day. The man was covered in blood and asked for a glass of water, after a long hike from town down the train tracks. But he put his axe down to drink the water. And in truth, you worry more about the loose-limbed moose that haunt your rural road, where the ditches bleed into the darkness of dusk and forest.

When you were younger and alone, you lived in the city in a high-rise. The bulky, tattooed biker you'd meet in the elevator told you he'd lost his leg in Vietnam. He had a new one made of plastic. "Come on, darlin'," he'd croon as the elevator rose. "Come on upstairs. Take off that leg o'mine and make sweet love to me."

A while later, someone kicked in your door and upended your bed and took off with the VCR in your dead grandmother's black suitcase. The cop who showed up said he didn't want to mess up your place by dusting for prints. Then he sat down in a comfortable chair in your living room and stayed for a good long while, as if he was looking for a wife.

*

At the Ghostkeeper Pub, your husband sings sweet and off-key. And you eat Nechako Nachos and wings and poutine and you say out loud, "I am happy," because it's a rare and precious feeling that's struggling to escape.

Tongue in the Wound

It was September and the sun was coming up when I heard the fear. A woman called the newspaper to warn us: "There are foreigners praying on top of the Peace River Dam." She said the Moslems were facing Mecca, faces down, foreheads down. Dawn. The dam. The hydroelectric dam past Hudson's Hope that holds back a flood-full of water. The woman spoke quietly. She demanded our publisher. She asked for a photographer. She almost whispered: "They're praying to Allah on the dam."

She heard it from the Mountie's wife she plays volleyball with at the old high school gym over in Grande Prairie, the one with the new flooring. They were playing volleyball just hours after the planes hit. I heard her fear.

We'd already heard that a small plane full of trophy hunters was fleeing the Omineca, speeding out of northern BC with their antlers and freezer meat. We'd heard the Pentagon was scrambling fighter jets to chase them as they sped south through empty sky.

What worried me more was the sound of my big, black dog Sam licking his belly in the dark on our bedroom floor. The *slup slup slup* of it. The abscess he opened in the night. The tongue in his wound. The sound that startled me awake. The suffering.

The morning the planes hit, I was due at the courthouse after an old man killed his white-haired lady friend in the alley behind Kentucky Fried Chicken. He shot her dead with his rifle, but I was delayed. I sat in front of the big TV in a corner of the tiny airport bar with a security guard who couldn't stop shaking. He kept describing a long-ago bomb that blew a plane right out of the sky over 100 Mile House. Now, we watched the towers fall on TV and the planes park outside, and I pulled out my reporter's notebook. All the miners bound for work up at Kemess Copper-Gold were stuck on the ground there with us, sweating on their duffle bags and swearing out loud. A stewardess was rolling her carry-on bag back and forth on its wheels, as if she was rocking her baby, and back home, my dog was dying on the living room floor.

By day's end, we determined the people praying on the Peace Dam were nothing but fiction. In truth, the commotion was from some hunters who were flagged down on Peace Dam Drive, where conservation officers armed with bear spray combed through their truck beds for fur and bones.

And my dog was about to die. Sam tried to fight back. He jerked and snapped at the vet who came to kill him. And after Sam was dead, I lay on the floor and hugged my dog's big, dead body and howled out loud, while my husband dug the grave out back, his shoulders heaving and shaking, knee-deep in the grave, and the sun going down.

Trumpener

Drag Marks

When I wake up, Farrell is nuzzling me, nibbling me. He says, "Mmmmmm." He licks my ear. He whispers, "I'll put the dogs out," as though it's foreplay.

I say, "No, better not. They'll get into Klaus' truck. They'll get into the skulls."

I say, "I'll take them out. We'll stay out of the forest. We'll stick to the road. And if some wild thing attacks, I'll beat it off with their leash."

"Beat it with the leash?" asks Farrell, rolling over. "Lucky beast."

There are so many new positions you have to learn when you live out here. Cradling your neck and playing dead if it's a grizzly. Walking backwards, eyes downcast, whispering softly for a black bear. Acting brash and larger than life against a cougar. I sometimes practise these precautions in my head as if they were the steps in a fire drill, or the first aid routine to stem fatal bleeding. But if it ever comes to that, I'm afraid I'll choose the wrong pose, or fumble with the bear spray, or forget how dead I'm supposed to play.

In the winter, it's always dark here and I walk the dogs rather desperately, along the side of the barbed-wire forest, the lights of the house and the red-eyed pump shack retreating behind me. I walk down to the bottom of the forest, along an old abandoned road covered in frozen shit and our footprints buried under Klaus' truck tires. The dogs disappear under the wire and it's hard to see your footfalls in the dark. The only path is the colour of snow.

*

We disagree on the dangers out there, Farrell and I, even though Klaus tried to warn us. Our landlord came to spend the night. He brought his wife, Anja, and their pumped-up truck packed down with animal skulls that were still alive with maggots and with the furs from his trapline on the Parsnip River. They were flying out to the winter markets back in Germany.

It was night outside, and we sat close together at the kitchen table. Our dogs, Samson and Lilly, lay on the brown, scuffed linoleum and teacups steamed in our hands and Klaus stroked his stocking feet across the top of the toes of his quiet bride.

Klaus told us we had to stay away from carcasses. He described the ragged circle of ravens we'd see in the sky, the cage of cow bones in the field beneath them, here a leathery leg still stuck to its hoof, there a half-smiling jaw bone. He told us the killer would be back to break the mouth of anyone hungry enough to feed. Anja laughed at that, and I waited for Farrell to sigh or disagree with him, but he didn't. I worried that perhaps we knew nothing about the harshness of this pastoral life, about the short, gasped screams of a rabbit carried away by a hawk. I felt I should get up and grab a pen and write warning notes on the skin of my hands. But when I made a move to get up, Klaus grabbed my arm. "Listen," he said. "This is vital." And I sat back down.

Klaus took a breath. "There is something much more dangerous that a carcass," he said. "A dead animal that's there—and then—suddenly gone. Look for the drag marks. Watch your back. The killer is in hiding, waiting to pounce."

Later, we all said good night.

In the morning, Farrell got up and made breakfast for our guests before they headed to the airport with their furs and bones. Klaus said he was hungry and I put out four spoons around the table but then Anja said she wasn't hungry or maybe she just shook her head. Farrell was cooking oatmeal on the stove with a wide metal spoon. He had his back to us. He didn't see how Klaus growled at his wife and faked a punch at Anja's face.

Sometimes you don't see it coming.

*

It's spring now and the thaw is giving up its dead. Our dog sniffs the raw air and bounds ahead of us in the light. Farrell and I follow, hand in hand, down the bush road. Farrell brings a tiny screwdriver to dig up rocks for his collection. But we find the dead calf first. A burst of red in the sunlight. Black-winged birds singing on a red rib and a patch of black fur, down in the ditch.

"Not pleasant," Farrell says, but anyway, he wants to look. He insists on it. I want to hurry home, but Farrell wants to dig. He finds a collared dog that's still stiff with winter and half-buried in the snow. I turn away and grab Lilly and kiss my dog flat on her snout. I squat on the road with my nose in Lilly's fur I don't even look for drag marks.

Honeymoon in the Dry Lands

Home

Our bedroom walls are streaked with the blood of bugs. Outside our window, the lumber mill throws up a purple glow of northern lights that catches a wasp hovering over lily pads in the swamp. In the daylight, the neighbour's kids fix their cat with a farm tool. They take asparagus for granted. Their parents boil the stalks until their kitchen smells sassy. I long for the fiddleheads we picked as newlyweds and cooked with such care, fried in the music of butter.

Bull Creek Canyon

I stand in front of the truck mirror and pluck blonde hairs from my chin. The sky above the campground curls like a bathing cap, with angelic blue around the edges, and hellfire orange inside. It withers from the day's long sun. Later on, after it's pitch dark, a Danish family tosses a blow-up beach ball from child to child between their tent and the outhouse. Police sirens race by going to the reserve. "Kid got it in the eye," they report at the gas station the next day. "Busted it up. Damn near lost his eye in his socket."

Lillooet

A policeman in a bulletproof vest sits with his back to the door of the restaurant. I slip inside, hoping to feed my ache for the grasslands. The officer turns and warns me to be careful. He tells me the utensils at the buffet are very hot. A worried waitress squats down next to him, holding the coffee pot just shy of his holster. She tells the constable she's lost a black kitten in the ducts of the hotel. Some kids were dangling it off the bridge. They were going to toss it over their heads into the Fraser when she ran up and begged for its life. But she had to bring the kitten with her to work, and now it's disappeared. The policeman sips his coffee. He says, "Leave 'er to me. My fortune cookie says your worries will soon be over."

Ashcroft

Her tiara is on the table, next to the ashtray in the cafe. Miss Ashcroft is wearing her sash and a blue velvet sleeveless gown and sitting in an orange booth. She's smoking. She's ignoring the two white-haired men in the next booth. I'm scribbling words down on white paper napkins.

"He was travelling in a tutu after his wife died."

"They had him screwed up so bad, he didn't know if he was the tooth fairy or Bugs Bunny or what."

"Your original problem might go away, but you got ten more."

"Got that right."

There's a pause. Miss Ashcroft takes a puff.

The conversation begins again.

"Drugged him up so bad, he thought he was the tooth fairy. Doctor had to shake him off all that crap."

"Like I told him: you don't have to buy the whole living room set. You don't have to buy the couch, the armchair, the side tables, and the lamp."

"Right. Right. You can just buy the couch, if that's all you need."

"That may be all you need."

Lee's Corner

Everything is hot and moving slow. German tourists and kids from Anahim are ducking into the general store for thick, white ice cream cones. The store cat has just dropped her second load of all-white kittens into the insulation at New and Used Furniture. "Some slinky, white-ass cougar tom" is all anyone will say about the father. Every car crossing over the Sheep Creek Bridge makes a soft sound like water in a glass.

33   Trumpener

Flood Watch

ong ago, your father was left alone outside in his baby carriage and almost drowned. At first, he lay there, watching the dark clouds float by. And when the rain blew in, he could feel the cool drops on his face and the water rising around him in the carriage. His mother remembers her baby's head in a puddle, his nose above water, or so the story goes.

These days, the rivers are coming up fast and brown and wide and you're still trying to get a breath. The day you speed out to Willow River, with your gumboot on the gas, men have stopped their trucks on the bridge to shake their heads and watch the tree debris dance in the drink. The ditches are creeks and the creeks are ponds and the rivers are lakes. And a beautiful girl rows out in her mother's metal boat to ferry you up the driveway. You hear the oar sipping water and the dogs howling from the attic. You hear the distress calls of geese, their eggs underwater, their nests out at sea.

A month later, and you're still watching the water. A black bear comes down from the hills by the pulp mill to sniff at the bank, and the muskrats swim by faster. The daycare kids in raincoats stand in a giggling line at Paddlewheel Park and wait for the Fraser to swallow their toes. Neighbours come down with bowls of oatmeal and berries to sit on park benches that will soon be swept away. Everyone remembers the year it was worse than Noah's Ark. They recall the flood that was worse than Usk, when the river swept away everything but the Bible in a tiny church. You hear spoons clinking oatmeal bowls and a roar from the river. You see a mound of sand waiting for shovels at the end of the street and a black dog racing a Frisbee into the flood. Parents snap pictures of their kids in the current. An old man leaves his trailer with a gallon jug of wine. And when the police finally march down Farrell Street to get people out of their houses, a cop with dry boots has to stop first to chase away the boys who are splashing in the gazebo and diving off the picnic tables.

Far away, to the west, there are mudslides and landslides and sandbags passed from hand to hand to hand. Dream homes and totem poles are swimming in the dark. There are rumours of a run on milk and a shortage of gas and a Great Wave that's bearing down on Kispiox.

You catch a ride into the flood zone in a blue truck, until the pickup stalls and starts filling with dirty water. You hold your hands above your head, as if that will save you. You escape to a house where the basement was flooded and everyone climbed upstairs. You sleep to the drone of generators and pumps. You dream of an old man dancing in rubber boots in the washout near Old Remo. The old man is dancing and crying and feeling the rain on his face.

Elk Canyon Bugler
Seeks Junior Reporter

W*hen* the mayor gets hit by a logging truck, you go. If a man tries to turn city hall into a snake pit display called The House of Yular, you bring your own camera. You bring your own mice. You feed the cobras behind the beaded curtain in Yular's dark basement. You use your flash.

When the grade school kids sing a ukulele song about Chi-Chi-the-Chihuahua at their jamboree, you get their names. When a drunk from Dry Grad takes an axe to the Hindu family's apple trees, you pick up the branches. When your editor slips out for quick, secretive sex in the rusty beehive burner at valley bottom, you write the headlines.

You take your lunches. You monitor the police scanner.

When the police dispatcher reports drunks having sex in the bush by the Legion, you go. When a scrawny grizzly gets shot on the bridge, you capture her orphaned cubs, small as dogs. When a police officer holds up a girl's tiny panties as Exhibit A in the courthouse, you write it up.

When a logging truck jackknifes on Plateau Crossing in the worst April snowstorm, you wade through the drifts to find the driver. You wipe the wet flakes from your camera on the highway's soft shoulder.

If you have to cry, you cry at home.

When a diver drowns trapped in the drain at the bottom of the pulp mill pond, you take your car. If a house burns in winter on the steep side of the canyon, you bring your mittens and a pencil that still writes in the cold. You watch the firemen's boots slide downhill all night on the ice their hoses made. You wash the ashes from your hair.

When it's autumn, you cover the garden sculptures and the knapweed display and the vegetable competition at the fall fair. You praise the place that takes time to honour the longest green bean in town.

The Red Tide

The *bad* kids in McBride lean out of their truck and shout, "Mount Robson's on the rag!" at the blood-red trees that skirt the park. Motorists from Michigan eat blueberry bagels in the front seat. They drive towards Vanderhoof, delighted that the north has such pretty fall colours all year long.

In my neck of the woods, I watch thick bush wrestled into mud bog and slash heaven. In winter, I drive home past pyramids of yellow flame, strings of abandoned campfires licking the night air as they blaze across a dark field. I watch the cattle move in, with their big dull eyes, and the deer nibble up to the side of the road and then skit away, in search of cover.

Long ago, we could only see what was happening if we were up in the sky. Flying back north, we all pressed our noses against the tiny airplane windows, making startled sounds with our tongues, or shaking our heads. Later, we saw red right along the roads to Hixon and Houston and we'd fret about it as we paid for gas in Quesnel or Vanderhoof. These days, Prince George is playing strip poker in the pines and she's lost her shirt and she's showing a lot of skin. She reveals things I'd never noticed before:

gravestones, schoolyards and neighbourhoods that used to hide in the shade. Now, we can watch the death throes in our own backyards as we wash the burned bits from the soup pot in the kitchen sink. One man shows me the trees he's losing, the track marks left behind. His eyes are red, as if there's been a death in the family.

Politicians and lumbermen stand up and damn the Red Tide. They carry a model of a pine beetle as big as my dog. They say, "That's one big honking pine beetle." Their speeches log the words catastrophe, emergency, and unprecedented natural disaster. They use terms like infestation and epidemic and biblical plague. They chart the spreading stain of the mountain pine beetle on larger and larger maps. They name a Beetle Boss. They launch a War in the Woods. They plan to bring in an army of woodpeckers.

We listen for the flight of the beetle and the sound of all those tiny wings on the wind. We imagine the taste of what they nibble, the heat of their potent procreation, and the blush of blue fungus they leave behind. We try tough love. We inject our trees with arsenic to kill the pine and starve the beetle, just like the nursery rhyme.

> *She swallowed the bird to eat the spider,*
> *who wiggled and wriggled and tickled inside her.*
> *She swallowed the spider to catch the fly.*
> *I don't know why she swallowed the fly.*
> *I guess she'll die.*

We dream of drowning beetle wood under water or burning it beneath our sidewalks. We try to repel the bugs with a smelly bag of pheromones that looks like Swiss cheese and hangs on the trees. We repeat the word pheromone, because we like the sound. Other words are less pleasing, like annual cuts and logging uplifts and the coming downfall. We dig up the words red and dead. We watch them rot. We hold our breath. We wait for the words to run dry, when the forest lies dead on the floor.

Slices

I *used* to work in a kitchen. I cooked up lunch for mill workers who sat down to eat with grit on their gums. They blasted their clothes with a quick kiss of compressed air. They washed their hands at a long, steel sink. They smelled sweet to me, like sawdust and pine. They piled their hard hats under the dining hall tables. They dropped their earplugs by their forks. And rows and rows of men in blue shirts and blue pants and big boots would lean their arms on the tables and look up at us in the kitchen, eager to eat.

My kitchen was a sauna of drains and hoses and steam and big, boiling pots that smelled like sour noodles. My job was to whip up trays of fresh vegetables. I'd haul out huge wooden crates of tomatoes and peppers still sweating from the cold room. I'd drop them into soapy water in a deep sink and watch them pop back up. I'd dry the tomatoes and the peppers and cut them open. I'd rip out the seeds and slice them and fit them piece by piece into long, metal trays.

I was good at my job and I was fast, way faster than the lady doing lettuce. Still, I complained a lot. Once I could do the job,

I could do it. No mystery or surprise, just ripe slices, faster and faster, knocking out the seeds and laying them soft and gentle On the metal tray. So that day in spring, when they decided to transfer me out to the wood shop floor, I was excited. I hung up my wet apron and felt like a pioneer.

My new job was like this: I branded hammer handles. I pounded peg noses into wooden duck toys. I smoothed the ends of long, wooden broom handles in a huge machine with a vibrating hole. At lunch, I blasted the sawdust off my clothes with the air hose and I washed my hands and I sat down to eat raw peppers and stew. Then I put my hard hat back on and stuck in my earplugs. I went back out to pound peg noses and brand hammer handles and stick long poles into a vibrating Vise-Grip.

I was the second woman ever hired on at the wood shop. The other one was old enough to have grey hair in a bun. She told me the men didn't like having girls there, because they stank of perfume. She wore a dress and a white glove that covered up the finger stubs on her hand. She had lost four of her fingers, but I never asked her how. She sat at a desk underneath a big old clock and answered the black, rotary telephone. She paged the boss over the intercom with very long vowels. "Frankeeeeeeee! Telephoooooone!" She never dialed out.

We worked with a man who was missing a fingertip. He would rub the stub along his shiny, black moustache. Or he'd aim his amputated finger at his crotch and laugh. My boss once squashed his own thumb in the hydraulic compressor, but he never laughed about it. And one morning, a foreign worker grabbed me by my shoulder and pretended to jab a splinter of wood into his own eyeball. He grabbed at his face and clawed at his eye and pretended to cry and then he laughed out loud. Other than that, everyone pretty much ignored me. After a few months, one guy did warn me to tie back my long hair, so I wouldn't get scalped by a machine. I thought that was nice of him.

At lunch, I'd crunch raw peppers and watch the women slip on puddles in the steamy kitchen. Then I'd go back and pound peg noses into wooden ducks. I'd smooth the ends of long wooden poles. I'd brand hammer handles. I was glum. Over the noise of the machines, my boss yelled, "No one ever said hard work would be interesting!"

Finally, my boss sent me to work on the circular saw. I spent hours on the circular saw. I sawed in fear, in a cold sweat, with my eyes shut tight. I spent days of my life moving that quicksilver blade through obstinate wood. I turned long pieces of wood into shorter pieces of wood. I turned shorter pieces of wood into tinier pieces of wood.

Winter came and the kitchen began serving more potatoes and fewer tomatoes. They still served trays of red and green peppers. I blew sawdust off my clothes. I washed my hands.

Spring came and there was even more wood stacked up in the mill yard, waiting. I was still wary of the saw, with its flying slivers and biting blade. But I finally decided the slow arms on the wood shop clock were much more dangerous than that saw blade. I wondered how it would feel if I just eased that saw right through my pepper of a hand and laid it gently on a tray.

Trumpener

She's Light on Her Feet and She Lets the Man Lead

W*e bought* the huge king-sized bed that wouldn't fit up the stairs from our country dance teacher. She's the one with the silver high heels and sturdy calves and the commission job in furniture sales. She sells us the king bed that comes with a free DVD and then she tries to tack on mattress pads and seal coating. I tell her good luck. I tell her we got our first marriage bed cheap at the auction in Williams Lake. It used to be a hotel bed at the Overlander, double-wide and extra long. A million eager cowboys must have whipped out their lassoes and rounded up some romance in our bed. I tell her we don't need any more protection than that.

She doesn't hold it against us. She's light on her feet and she lets the man lead. She tells us that's how you do country dance. She urges me to give up my arm to my husband and let him dance me backwards, blind and trusting. She counts us around the dance floor with "Quick-quick. Slow. Slow."

After we buy the bed at the Boxing Day Sale, our country dance teacher sends us off to practise our two-step at the Cariboo Country Hall New Year's Dance and Midnight Buffet. She tells us to turn left at Quesnel and drive into the mountains to dance and eat some mayonnaise salads.

And we're all dressed up and ready to go with the dog in the back, when we discover the dog's neck smells like moose leg. And so my husband heaves the dog out of the car and carries him down to the basement and bathes him with my special moisturizing soap. And the whole drive out, my husband is murmuring gentle things to soothe that moist black dog.

Now, dogs aren't allowed at the New Year's party in the tiny town with the wooden hall where a short Mountie at the door stamps your hand and offers you free refills on coffee. The dogs have to stay behind in a low motel with skinny towels. Our damp black dog lies down in Room 8 for an Auld Lang Syne snooze and we hike back up to the hall to get stamps on our hands and cups of coffee.

Inside, four old boys in a band are twanging up on stage. There's a halo of blinking Christmas lights. Out on the dance floor, the gold company guys are keeping their girls awake with tight, slow dances and a tall woman in an elf hat is leading a circle dance with toddlers in mukluks. Girls who've tip-tapped their way down the Goat River Trail kick off their hiking boots. My husband slips out to check on the dog, and another fellow sidles on over to tell me he's been thinned out by blastocyte parasites from the Bowron. He's staying in the rooms above the saloon and we get up to dance, but I'm not good at letting him lead.

At midnight, my husband and I fumble around the floor for awhile, but we soon give up. The hometown crowd is putting out salads with creamy dressings and devilled eggs, and ladies with long forks dance over meat trays and hand out turkey and ham at the head of the table. There's Creedance Clearwater Revival on the dance floor and "Get it On, Bang a Gong" and then they bring out pie and Nanaimo bars.

We stumble home full of resolutions to dance more next year. The motel dogs come out for the first sniff of the year, and they howl at the stars and the whining snowmobiles, and we shout "Happy New Year!" Just past the bright parking-lot lights are silent meadows and the icy cone of a volcano. But I can't sleep in the narrow motel bed, with my husband snoring and the dog huffing on the floor.

I sleep in the back seat with the dog while my husband drives us slowly home. And the next morning, he has to tear out the ceiling to waltz our big, new, king-sized bed up the stairs.

After Birth

The great thing about morning sickness is that wild animals are always hungry. When I puked outside in the morning, it was all licked clean by the time I got back. At first I thought it was my sweet husband with a bucket and a cloth, but then they sent William up north to fix the digester during a mill shutdown. He lived up there for months in trailers packed with guys willing to stay as long as the camp cook fried their bacon crisp and they didn't have to deal with their wives. At night, William would drop quarters and loonies into the pay phone and we'd talk about lots of nothing until all the coins dropped. Once, I looked up from our call and saw a small cinnamon bear run by my bedroom window.

The husbands were supposed to go to birth class with us, so they'd know what to do when the shit hit the fan. Every other man sitting on the birth class floor was loving up his lady's belly and milky breasts and kissing her sweet, ripe mouth. But my husband wasn't around to marvel as my stretch marks turned into icy skid marks like the ones on Beaver Forest Road.

The midwife told us the uterus is the biggest muscle in a

woman's body. She pulled out a weird, long, striped hat, like something from Dr. Seuss. She said, "Pretend this hat is your uterus, and these coloured stripes are your muscles." And before our very eyes, she stretched and squeezed that long, striped hat until a doll's head peeked out the far end, and one guy yelled, "Ouch!"

Those birth classes left me dog-tired, but I still couldn't sleep. After I'd talk with William, I'd go walk the dog in my pajamas. My pajama bottoms snagged on barbed wire fences and I'd go back to bed with burrs and bits of ice stuck to my ankles. Once, I left Sassy's leash up a moose blind I'd climbed just to see what I could see. The sky was flat and grey, like a short story set in Ontario. That night, I dreamed I found a pacifier in my purse.

I kept at it in birth class, breathing like a horse or belly dancing on my knees. I rolled yellow tennis balls against the wall with the small of my back. One night, I woke up suddenly in the dark and remembered where I'd left Sassy's leash. I wondered what my baby would look like and how bad the pain would be.

I knew William had more experience, because he'd helped deliver a calf. When he was a little kid, he wandered into the neighbour's barn and discovered a little bundle of calf legs sticking out of a cow. He ran to get the farmer and helped pull the calf out with a rope. After that, the farmer called him "Dr. William." He said, "Dr. William, a rope is quite something. Some farmers have to use chains and tractors to get 'em unstuck!" And one night, when William called me from the pay phone, I told him to race home with some chains and start up the tractor, because it was time.

My medical records called me "a tired, well-hydrated lady"

asking for morphine during "arrestive labour." But I guess the medical records left out the real story, starting with the cheese popcorn I was eating the night my water broke, or the birch tree I braced against, or how lonely that pain was. No one wrote down the moment I jumped out of bed and shouted to my dog, "Sassy, I guess you and me are having this baby alone."

No one recorded how many times I threw up, first into the glass salad bowl we got as a wedding present, second into the snow, then a dozen times into the hospital's moon-shaped turquoise Tupperware, and finally, into an anaesthetist's suction in the operating room.

The doctors didn't describe the snowy treetops against the dark sky out the back window on the way to hospital. They didn't mention the ugly contraction I slammed through by singing into the doors of Emergency, while two cops and a patient in handcuffs watched me.

They forgot to write down the way the hands of the clock went around and around and around, another morning, another afternoon, another evening, long hours that took me farther and farther away from remembering I was supposed to have a baby.

No nurse recorded the exact details of the decision to cut that baby out of me or why it inspired me to brush my teeth. There's nothing about William's tractor jokes, or how handsome my husband looked in blue surgical scrubs. The records forgot the seventeen staples left in my stomach and the men in masks juggling my intestines to shimmy my daughter out. They didn't mention William cutting the cord that was tough as calamari. There was no diagram of the way my arms were stretched wide as if I was nailed to a cross, so I couldn't hold my baby at all.

While they sewed me up with boat rope as thick as your arm, I pressed my nose against her big-eyed face and whispered, "I love you, I love you."

The maternity ward was full of women with bikini cuts. We walked the halls in our bathrobes, bent over like half-opened penknives. We shuffled our babies in clear bassinets down the dingy halls until our milk came in like daggers, and then they sent us home.

We snuck out of the hospital with a snippet of our baby's bloody umbilical cord that a nurse had stashed for us in a sandwich bag on ice. We kept the cord in the door of the fridge. We figured if William didn't have to go back up north to work, we'd bury it in the backyard after spring thaw. We'd have a little birth ceremony. But that never happened. Because the power failed in a huge storm and when we opened the fridge to salvage our food, the dog ate the baby's umbilical cord in all the commotion.

Pop Goes the Weasel!

A *wild,* white weasel came waltzing across our kitchen floor. He wouldn't leave. Outside, he'd seemed much sweeter, frolicking with his pale-haired partner around the garage. Even when the weasels followed the smell of garbage and crawled into the front seat of our car with the bad muffler for a noisy trip to the dump, we didn't really mind. It made for a good story. "Ermine," my husband had said, satisfied.

It was a feral time for us all. Our freshly born baby was teething and biting and bucking. My husband was working late every night, coming home in fire-retardant coveralls, his hair clotted with pulp. Meanwhile, the weasel was scouring our walls for mice. He left dry, twisty turds and triangular puddles in every room. I could smell him. And I could never let go of my baby, because weasels suck the blood right out of baby chicks.

> *Round and round the mulberry bush*
> *The monkey chased the weasel*
> *The monkey thought 'twas all in fun*
> *Pop! goes the weasel!*

The Internet called my weasel a "fearless fighter who attacks victims many times larger than himself." The neighbours offered me a mousetrap. My father told me to set a trap with fresh meat. My baby was learning to chew her own toes. I was weeping on the front porch. "Relax," said my husband, wiping black grit from his face. "The weasel will catch all the mice in the house and then he'll disappear." And then he went back to work.

I got frantic. I called the mayor. I called the other neighbours. I called the exterminators. The pest people said they're happy to kill rats and cockroaches, but they bow down in the face of a weasel. They advised me to barricade myself in a room with my baby and a shovel until my husband got home.

I called the distress centre. The volunteer counselor told me he had a weasel in the house that used to run across their shoulders at night. They set live traps with cans of fish bait until their whole house smelled like a cannery. They finally caught the weasel in a rat trap, but it ran around the house dragging the trap on its back. Finally, the vegetarian in the family had to slay the weasel with a block of wood.

My MP didn't answer. I called the government. At first, they were too busy laughing to help me. Then they said they were too busy with grizzly bears and poachers. My MLA told me to leave a trail of cat food for the weasel to follow right out my door. I was about to hitchhike to town with my baby to buy cat food when I got a call back. It was an angel of mercy, disguised as a government secretary. She offered to come over to our house after work with a live trap and bait.

Pamela told me she once helped a woman with a squirrel loose in her house. "She was terrified," she said. Pamela helped the woman close the curtains and contain the perimeter. Then she put on oven mitts and captured the snapping squirrel in her hands.

Pamela stood in my living room and listened. She said, "I think I hear him!" We set a live weasel trap and baited it with Friskies Chunks Chicken Dinner in Gravy. We sat down to wait. Pamela held my baby and soothed her while something wild tickled the walls around us.

Trumpener

Radiation

The cancer hospital leaves out small balls of yarn and a basket of knitting needles in the waiting room. "For people with too much time on their hands," you explain to your father. "Or too little!" he grunts back.

You begin to knit while your father waits beside you in his blue hospital bathrobe. You don't know quite what to make. Click, click, click, the needles rub up against each other, poking in and out of the loops of wool. Your father tells you he has the biggest prostate in all of Alberta. One of the biggest, anyway, his doctor told him. Your father is proud of that, in his own way. You picture a hard, red, rubber ball, like a clown's nose. Every afternoon, you pick up the knitting needles as your father lies down in a white room beneath a big machine. He opens up his blue bathrobe. He shows the technicians the black felt pen tattoos drawn on his hard, round belly, the arrows that show them where to shoot.

You drove here to the hospital over the mountains. Your backwards-facing baby watched home disappear. Near Tête Jaune Cache, your baby ate fingerfuls of banana and fistfuls of pine cone. At Lake Annette, you carried her past the "Quick-sand!" warning sign to count felt-horned elk. In Jasper, you watched giddy young girls with bare bellies climb up on metal bike racks to peek in the window of the Athabasca, where K-OS was warming up in the bar. "K-OS," you told your baby, pointing inside. "Chaos!" She woke up the next morning bigger, longer, even more your child.

In the hospital cafeteria, you find your mother eating mashed potatoes. "I got poisoning as a girl," she tells you, putting down her fork, "from picking wild sweet peas. The poison travelled all the way up my arm."

Your father hasn't been in hospital since the last emergency, when they operated on his heart. The sky back then was black and blue, winter before dawn, your plane rising and landing, rising and landing, the snow blowing across the runway as they sawed open his ribs. By the time you got there, your father's chest was zipped shut again, and you couldn't remember what you'd wanted to say to him.

Now, every afternoon in the waiting room of the cancer hospital, you pick up a new, small ball of yarn and start all over again. You never quite know what you're making or who will finish it.

The Way Muskox Bend to Gentle Herding

Your daughter puzzles over the white crayon that leaves no mark on her paper. She draws and draws and declares the crayon broken. She makes plans to bury it in the snow. She kisses you goodbye.

You surrender your vanilla yogurt to airport security and skim low over clouds and valleys in the belly of a plane that sweats and shakes as it drops down into the Yukon. You've flown north to Whitehorse to knock on the door of a painter who speaks only in metaphor. You want to learn how to scrape the hair off a muskox and use knitting needles made of bone.

Your daughter wants to be like the kids in this town, who stay up late to dance in their snow pants on gym mats in a cavernous white tent by the river. The tent smells like diesel and the children jump to live music, their mittens dancing around them on strings. The floor dancers visiting from Iqaluit spin on their shoulders and moon-walk. They mime a seal hunt. The teenage girls from Arviat lay their hands on each other's arms and sing duets with their throats, singing mouth to mouth, sharing the air. They stop only when they collapse into giggles at the sounds they've made of a bee and a buzz and the sharp crack of ice. The river outside steams in the cold. You walk back to your hotel bed in a cold so fierce it numbs your toes.

In the morning, a smiling family of servers takes turns running bacon and coffee and sunny-side-ups to your restaurant table. They bring you the newspaper, even though the headline exposes their father as Crazy Al, an alleged drug runner. The newspaper says Crazy Al is only pretending to bring noodles here from Vancouver in his white cube van. "How can you have a business just selling noodles?" demands the editorial. But you're only just starting to learn that all things are possible. That the world's best ski waxer makes his living here, and the dancer who choreographed a Parka Ballet. Years ago, a woman drove north to teach art to the kids in these schools. Now, she sits happily in the white tent by the river, making bowls out of pig gut and the milkweed pods her mother sends from Montreal. Nearby, Ruben is carving whalebone into high art and humming heavy metal in Inuktitut. Later on, he'll put down his air guitar to translate for the Whip Master of Nunavut. Back home, the Whip Master uses his long lash to slay ptarmigan to feed his family. He's come to this town to crack his whip and take down pop cans and slash cigarettes in half. People shout and clap. When the Whip Master's done, he coils up his whip and puts it away in a big, green garbage bag and then he collects his cheque.

That night, you fall asleep to the percussion of old-fashioned typewriter keys. You dream of raven puppets and the shadows they make in the sky. Somewhere in your hotel, a lounge singer in a tight silver dress is imitating sex and death with the sounds in the back of her throat. You are flying over a riverbank and rouse a moose up on its stumble legs. Below you are the hoofprints of goats and sharp blue ice. You fly over spruce-beetle ghost trees and fossil remains from the tsunami that swept down this valley and slammed into a mountain. You dream that muskox bend to gentle herding. All around you, the texture and light of snow that made a painter sick with metaphor.

Even a Blind Hen

Pirates

The winter you licked the frosty fence post to see how cold it tasted, you lost days of things you had to say.

*

At home, the nails in the roof were popping from the cold and we kids hid in the basement behind the furnace, sure the noise was robbers. Burglars, like the ones in the card trick my American Granny taught us, where you knocked four times on the roof of the house of cards and out jumped four robbers. They were stern jacks, with moustaches and swords. They scared you every single time, although Granny laughed and said she'd married worse. Now the robbers are stomping a warning on your frozen shingles: We are coming to get you.

Our parents have flown away to New Orleans to get me a pirate pencil with the face of a one-eyed man. We are sick from eating marzipan, and Cinders freezes the tips of her ears waiting under the bird feeder. The babysitter chases my sister around the kitchen until she cries. My brother asks the Ouija board if our parents' plane will crash and the answer comes back Y-E-S.

My mouth tastes like burnt tongue and I can't even call for help.

Pitchfork

Your father was harvested with a pitchfork. That's what he tells you. And he shows you the bumps of bone the pitchfork left behind. They're just below his bald spot. They feel strange, like the horns of a baby goat. You sit on the goat's lap and pet its head, but your mother steps in. "Oh honey," she says. "Your father was not harvested with a pitchfork. He was delivered with forceps. That's all."

"It was a pitchfork!" your father insists, cuddling you in his arms. "I was born with the scars to prove it." And then he laughs.

When your father snorts with laughter, his big nostrils get even wider. You smell salami and onion and radish on his breath. You stay on your father's lap and listen. He tells you his mother had to push so hard, she broke her tailbone getting him out. He tells you the boys from Hitler Youth used to call him Moses. He tells you a Russian soldier danced him against an alley wall. Your father twists his sad little stories and makes them so strange and funny that you forget to cry.

Your father bounces you on his knee. *Hoppe, hoppe Reiter!*

Wenn er fällt dann schreit er! It's a wild German game with a galloping horse.

> *Jump! Jump! Rider so tough!*
> *Your horse bucks you off and off and off*
> *When it's too much, you cry and cough!*
>
> *Oh, dear rider, please don't fall*
> *Your grave is cold and very small*
> *The ravens will peck your organs all.*

You saw ravens feasting once on a red stain of deer blood on the Yellowhead Highway, just past Obed Summit. Your father was driving. Your mother shouted, "Watch out!" You saw dark birds in the middle of the road, sipping from a bloody birthmark.

Your father protects you from the ravens. He gallops fast and he bucks hard, but he always catches you before you fall into your cold, small grave.

The Hard of Hears

After *Jack* crashed his bike with the banana seat roaring down Groat Road and got a steel plate in his head, he started throwing snowballs at the Hard of Hears at school. Jack took aim at the skinny kids who ran around with boxes of sound strapped to their hearts. Hard of Hears came from reserves up north. They were sent to classrooms at the farthest end of our school. Their teachers yelled. Their batteries squealed and whistled. The Hard of Hears talked with their hands and their eyebrows. We weren't allowed to go near them.

So we talked among ourselves, at our end of the schoolyard. We talked about Jack's bike crash, or why Larissa drew a Nazi swastika on a Pink Pearl eraser and threw it at my head. We talked about Carol-Anne's father burning her cheek with hot raisin toast, and throwing her out in the snow in her socks before school, and the mark it left on her cheek. We wondered why the popular girls in grade six got their dogs to chase us after school. The biggest girls would grab us and kick at their mutts and yell, "Sic 'em! Sic 'em!" until they barked at us.

But the week before Jack threw his ice ball, all we could

talk about was the kidnapping. The only millionaire on Groat Road made a lot of money selling bacon and growing his beard. His daughter was in Imps with me at Brownies. I'd hold her little hand and dance around the Toad Stool. Then some robbers broke into their mansion. They caught the millionaire napping and wouldn't let him leave. That night, we heard bullhorns and sirens and some of us hiked over to Groat Road with our parents. We set up lawn chairs in the traffic circle and sat under big blankets and watched. There were gunmen crouched behind police cars. Just as we were getting really cold, the police broke down the door. But they shot the millionaire by mistake, instead of the robbers. The millionaire made it out alive, but his daughter never came back to Brownies.

We never got to play with the Hard of Hears, either, until the day Jack started flinging snow at them one recess and we all joined in. It was the first time we ever had fun with the Hard of Hears. But then Jack threw an ice ball at someone's eye and the Hard of Hears' grumpiest teacher came galloping outside in her big, stomping boots. She was shouting and pulling and hauling her kids down off the snow hill. She pushed them all around her in a circle and made them read her lips. "Mittens off! Hands out! You are all getting the strap!" She was yelling and showing her teeth. We could hear well enough to run away in time, and no one ever blamed Jack for starting it, because he had a plate in his head.

No! No! No!

My *Oma* lay paralyzed where our dinner table used to be. She chanted, "Nein! Nein! Nein!" for hours. She could only move her mouth and her arm. She lifted her arm up in the air and then she dropped it. Up and down, up and down. "Nein! Nein! Nein!"

I'd sit next to her bed in our dining room, scratching my hands. My big brother called me Scary Skin and Hands of Hate because I was starting to lose my skin. My hands were red and dry and raw. When I picked up the funnies in the Saturday newspaper, the ink would melt the skin off my fingertips before I even got to read Family Circus. I'd turn on the tap in the bathroom upstairs. I'd let hot water thrum against the ink and the itch until I screamed.

"Hey, Third Degree," my brother would call up. "Dinner's ready!"

"Quit scratching," my sister would say during dinner at the kitchen table. "You got fleas or something?"

"You'll wind up with no skin at all!" my father warned.

"Please!" My mother would say.

"Nein! Nein! Nein!" my Oma would call from the dining room.

"Quiet!" my father would shout at her. "That's enough!"

After dinner, in my cold upstairs room I'd scratch at my fingers and pick at the scabs. I'd play with the ladder I got for Christmas. I was supposed to leave the ladder in its box until our house burnt down. But it was made of heavy chains that felt rough and cool against my skin. If I ever smelled smoke, my parents told me to pull out the ladder and hurl it at my icy window as hard as I could. I was supposed to climb out over the shards of glass and ice and climb down and make my getaway. Until that happened, I sat upstairs and used it as a scratching post.

My mother took me downtown on the bus to see a doctor. She told me this doctor was smart about many things, including lepers in Louisiana. The only lepers I knew were from Ben Hur. They lived in a cave until their noses fell off. They were mixed up in my mind with the chariot race scene where people were whipped bloody and crushed under carriage wheels.

At the medical clinic, I sat on a thin, crisp bed while an old man held my hands in his well-washed fingers. The skin doctor spoke English more strangely than my father. He turned my hands over and over and peered at the dead, angry skin. He closed his eyes and held my hands and called them *wadis*. "You have your own dry riverbeds running right through the Holy Land, my dear." He smiled. He didn't know what was wrong with me. He didn't have a cure. But his gentle hands gave me hope.

The doctor advised my mother to slather my hands in

petroleum jelly. By the time the snow melted that year, my father was complaining bitterly about all the greasy doorknobs in the house.

In spring, they tried something new. My parents would drag me up the stairs howling. They'd pin me down on the bathroom floor while I screamed. "We're holding you down with hands of love!" my father would shout. I'd listen to my Oma chanting as my parents wrapped my hands in corn starch and white rags. They'd wait awhile. Then they'd pull off the rags and rip up my scabs. They'd rub medicine in the wounds. They'd look for signs of healing.

My sister's gym class found a belt and panties in the bushes while they were running in the ravine. No one knew if it was evidence of love or violence and my sister was excited and afraid and her gym teacher called the police. My mother sent my sister and me to kung fu class, so we could fight back. Also, my sister wanted to meet boys. We came home covered in bruises. We practiced kung fu by my Oma's bed and my Oma would move her arm up and down in a different rhythm. My Oma would smile at us and hum. There we were, my sister and I, kicking and blocking and fighting for our lives, and my Oma thought we were dancing.

Snow Angels

It's winter and your bedroom window is thick with ice. Downstairs, you drink black milk in the dark. Long icicles hang from the roof by their fingernails and your father knocks them down with a red shovel and hands them to you, sharp end first. You suck the cold all the way to school.

The Irish janitor sits in his hot furnace room that smells of boiled soap, by the Boys' Entrance. You step in the puddles your boots made. You walk home at dusk along the tops of huge snow hills left by the plows. A boy from school slips behind you and follows you home. He chases you. He pounces when you slip and fall. He beats your face with his red toque until your nose bleeds just one drop. One day, this boy will hang himself from a tree in his mother's front yard.

One day, you'll write a story about what really happened, about the boy's front yard and the crabapple tree and the weeping willow. You'll write a story about the oil boom and the wave of American hiring and the young professors who put their babies and books into cardboard boxes and drove their wives north across the border, heading along the flat prairie past Nisku.

You'll write about their disappointment. You'll write about the new professors' houses, built sharp with glass, and their wives sitting inside their new stucco homes. You'll write about the children growing up in darkness. You'll write about their mothers' campaign to get rid of the dark and save their kids. You'll write about the girl leaping from her window and the mimeographed notices sent home in mittened hands and the Saturday bottle drive fundraisers. You'll write about your mother pulling off her gloves and touching every last chilly finger on both her hands to count all the neighbourhood children found hanging or falling or slipping from life.

Your bedroom window is thick with ice. Outside, on the snowy sidewalk, a drunken man lunges at your father. He grabs for the shovel and knocks your father off his feet. Your father falls to the ground. He looks up at the sky and moves his arms a little, as if he's making a snow angel. It's winter and the ground slips out from under.

Trumpener

Nazis

E*very* morning, my sister and I beat the dark night out of our feather beds. We hang our bed covers over the balcony railing. Clara and I take turns whipping the evil out with a walking cane. I'm still afraid of the dark, so my sister curses our bedding with pretend German swear words. "Schicklegrubber! Sauerkrautschimpfen! Blutanfang!" She tries to make me laugh. We curse and hit our soft covers. The puffs of dust make me cough and sneeze. Clara hisses, "Gesundheit, Schnuckiputz!" until I get the giggles. Then we go back to whispering. Clara always has lots to tell me about. She warned me about the sickness that put Roman Schiller in hospital and killed the baker's grandmother. When we got to Germany, she told me our house really belonged to the children of old Nazis. She put her finger against her lips and said, "Shhhhhh."

When the big church bells interrupt us, it's time for Clara to go to school. She pulls on her knee socks and sandals and straps a big leather briefcase to her back and climbs our fence into the farmer's field. She walks beside the cow pasture and the manure pile and I watch her get smaller and smaller until she finally disappears behind the huge village church. Clara calls it the Heavenly Church. There are big, golden gates around the altar and fat, pink angels playing on the ceiling. When his grandmother died, the baker sat below the angels and cried so loudly we could hear him from the back pew. Later on, they planted his Oma in the backyard of the church.

We see the baker every morning when he brings fresh buns to our front door. I watch his face to see if he's still crying about his Oma, or if he's fallen sick. His face is very red, but he still looks cheerful. He always knocks on our door and shouts, "Grüss Gott!" Everyone shouts "Greet God!" when they see you, just to be friendly. Except for my mother. She mostly speaks English, so she just takes the buns from the baker and smiles and closes the door. My father is right behind her in his necktie and big, black glasses, ready for work. As soon as the front door closes, my father pulls the bag of buns out of my mother's hands and shouts, "Wash your paws, for God's sake!"

My father washes his hands a lot. He drives past the farmer's field and the church. He goes down the mountain and into the city to the library. He reads through old boxes of papers to find out why there was a war. His hands get very dusty.

After my father goes to the library and Clara goes to school, I drink the rest of my milk and eat the soft part of my bun. I chew until the bread gets sweet and then turns sour. I slam the front door and chase some bees around the yard. I drag my hand along the farmer's fence until I grab stinging nettles by mistake. I run crying to my mother, but she's already mad because she found my bun crust under the table. I go stick my stinging hands in the toilet. After awhile, I go out to look at ants and dry my hands in the sun.

When it's time to go pick up Clara at school, I follow my mother. Down past the manure pile, into the village. I hang on to the bottom of my mother's shopping bag to hide from the street sweeper with the bristle broom. In front of the Heavenly Church, old men are playing chess, but their chessboard is bigger than our backyard. The chess pieces are giant, bigger than soldiers. The old men have to crouch down just to lift up their castle and pawns. They sweat and shuffle as we wait for Clara.

At school today, Clara learned to crochet a pillowcase with green wool that they'll send to Roman Schiller in hospital. The hairdresser's daughter taught Clara some more new words in German. Before lunch, everyone had to line up and do the long jump.

"Crouch and swing your arms, just like this! That's it!" Clara shows me while we wait in the church square for our mother to buy tomatoes and sausage and soap. She takes so long that Clara starts to teach me the song with the missing word they learned in class—

> *Jetzt fahren wir übern See. Übern See*
> *jetz fahren wir übern See.*
> *Jetzt fahren wir übern See, übern See*
> *jetzt fahren wir übern ____*

—and then they'd all take a big breath and pull that last word back, hold it in, choked back, all of them, holding back the See.

We crossed the ocean to get here, on a big ship with its own movie theatre. My mother got seasick and took to her bunk. My father was making notes about wars. Clara and I would sway our way through the big ship. We'd press the elevator call buttons and run away before it came. We'd hide in the movie theater, where it was dark and cool. I would sit holding Clara's hand and weep about Bambi's dead mother. After that, Clara and I spent our time in the saltwater swimming pool, instead. Or we'd stick our noses against the porthole and watch the grey water.

. When we got to our new house in my father's old country, there were strangers inside, a man and a woman with big smiles. They washed their hands and fed us cake and whipped cream on little plates. They hugged me and gave me a green bear named for a cough medicine. They showed me the bear and pretended to cough loudly into their fists, trying to explain his name to me without words.

They sent Clara and me over the fence to the farmer's house with a metal pail, even though it was almost dark. We could barely speak to the farmer, but his daughter waved for us to follow her. Their cow lived right in the basement of their house. The cow had her very own low room that smelled like the bathroom. The farmer's daughter pulled the milk right out of the cow and poured it in our pail.

It was hard to get the milk pail over our fence. Clara whispered to me that the people sitting in our new house were the children of old Nazis. I was scared, but she told me it was all over now. My mother hated the cow's milk. She called it bitter. She put me to sleep under a feather bed with my new green Hustinetten bear. I begged her to leave the lights on.

*

The day my sister ran home from school crying, I was already sick on the floor. Clara rubbed my head and cried while my mother called for help. The village doctor was busy until nightfall, that's what my mother understood. My mother made up new German words on the telephone, trying to get him here sooner. The doctor ordered a sweat cure for us, until he arrived.

My mother wrapped Clara and me in flannel nightgowns and housecoats and all the blankets and feather quilts in the house. She plugged in a vaporizer and turned up the heat and stuck steaming bowls of water in our room and closed the door. Clara and I lay in our cocoons and sweated. My sister kept on crying about the film they showed at school. She was so upset, she didn't care about whispering. She told me about men as skinny as Hallowe'en skeletons bent over barbed wire and bodies stacked up like firewood. She cried so hard she couldn't catch her breath, until we finally fell asleep, still cold and hot and wet and steaming with sweat. When I woke up, the doctor was standing by my bed. I could see him with the light from the hallway. My mother was struggling to come up with the words to thank him. She was so grateful he came to help us. She was trying to tell him that he was spoiling us with all his care and concern. She didn't know how to say it right. She told the doctor, "You are ruining us. You are ruining my children."

Even a Blind Hen

The *Germans* have a saying for everything. Proverbs your father served up suddenly at dinner, short and sharp: *Shöne Beine hat das Pferd!* Admiring your mother, bending at the stove: The horse has nice legs!

Years later, you poke at these with your English tongue, looking for a peck of truth: *Selbst ein blindes Huhn findet ein Korn.* Even a blind hen finds a kernel of corn.

Your baby wakes before the rooster crows and takes you by the finger to the chicken coop across the gravel road, where the birds are ruffled up together, dreaming of a scoop of dry corn and the fat-leafed weeds you pass through the wire. Nearby, the long-snouted dog is asleep in the grass. He's been stalking the birds for weeks, racing their shadows along the fence. Inside, the hens start to peck at the small black quail and the rooster starts beaking on the hens, holding them down by the neck and finishing up with just a few flaps.

Am Abend werden selbst die Faulen fleißig. At night, even the lazy get busy.

Your daughter gathers tiny brown eggs no bigger than her

hands. She carries them home past the laundry draped over the fence and the thistles and the burdock. She carries one egg in each hand across the gravel road, two eggs for you to boil, and sometimes she'll squat down in the gravel and look for bugs. Later, she'll watch you crack an egg in the pan, or she'll tap it on the floor and peel it, or bless it with salt.

But this morning, she busts her egg on the snout of the dog: Even a canine can crack an egg! The surprised wet snout. The dog's snarl. The shells in your daughter's hands. *Kleinvieh macht auch Mist.* Small beasts can still make big shit.

Instructions for Altar Boys

General Conduct

- *Walk with hands held in front unless carrying something*

I *carry* the cross. Pastor Rick follows me with the communion wine on this solemn hike. Everyone follows us down the path through the forest. At Beauty Lake Bible Camp, we get up before dawn to pray to God by the swimming docks. We hike to the sunrise service in the clearing, where I lean the cross against a tree. We all make a circle and hold hands and drop our heads. God smells like pine needles and the dirt on my hands.

We kneel on the forest floor to pray for Tracy's sick cousin. We pray for Dirk, our new Youth Group leader. We ask God to give speedy passage to secret bibles hidden in station wagons bound for Russia. We pray for the Soviets to learn His Truth. We cry for Mona, the Baha'i girl hanged in Iran, and for Chileans singing sad folk songs inside barbed wire, and then pretty soon it's time for archery.

In the afternoon, we turn pine cones into prayer shawls with a hot glue gun. I wear my prayer shawl when I lead the processions. At Beauty Lake Bible Camp, I carry the cross down the path or up the chapel aisle, and Pastor Rick follows, and Dirk's Youth Group, and the choir, and then everyone else. I serve Pastor Rick at the altar, even though that used to be a boy's job and I'm a girl. I'm not even in junior high yet, but I still get to wear the altar boy's robe and the pine-cone prayer shawl and light the candles in the woods. Dirk from Youth Group sometimes gives me the thumbs-up from his seat in the chapel or on the forest floor. And I get to call out the hymn numbers and bring out the bread.

The bread is the Body of Christ. You're supposed to let his skin melt on your tongue, but I'm usually too hungry. I like the crunch of the Communion wafers, so Christ doesn't last long. It's too bad, because I really love Jesus H. Christ a lot, and not just because he's cool and also good-looking. Jesus looks like a really nice tree planter to me, even though I don't like scratchy beards. I've heard his mother, Virgin Mary, is also quite nice. His father did renovations and construction. Dirk says if the Bible was written today, Joseph might be driving the Holy Family around in a camper and looking for work in Fort McMurray.

Wherever he lives, I respect the body of Christ. But Christ's-Blood-Given-for-You in that tinny Communion chalice is just plain sour. No matter how bad it tastes, though, you're not supposed to make a face. Up at the altar, everybody's watching and you better act quite holy. It's one of the rules.

> ### During the Service
> • *Refrain from too much gazing around
> while sitting at the front of the church*

We're not supposed to look around during church. But it's hard to stop gazing at Dirk's wife. She sings very sweetly. She kneels in her choir robes and opens her thin lips for Communion. She watches quietly with her round glasses and listens to the Word of God. God's the one who knows what happened. But Dirk's wife doesn't know I saw what's beneath her choir robes. Dirk keeps those pictures in old photo albums with sticky pages. He told me his wife likes to take off her glasses, even though she's got a small chest and a bird's nest between her legs. "What can I say?" Dirk said to me. "My wife loves wearing nothing but a smile."

My friend Tracy says it doesn't matter. She still likes Dirk. He never makes us do lame Bible study. He has fairly good ideas for an adult, like having the First Annual Youth Group Chapel Sleepover. We get to stay up late in the small chapel on Saturday night and eat Old Dutch chips in our sleeping bags and we won't have to read about lepers or Genesis.

Dirk told us that when he was a little boy, his Sunday school teacher always read them cheerful stories about God's love. She got them to colour bright rainbows over Noah's Ark. She insisted no one drowned in the flood or died on the cross. "All I'm saying," Dirk tells us, "is the Bible isn't just happy, yappy stories."

But I'm happy at Beauty Lake. At night, we square dance in

the lodge until Natalie pees her pants from laughing so much while coming 'round the outside. We eat fistfuls of slippery buttered popcorn and drop stray kernels into the green velour couches. We sink into the cushions and vow we'll never swear or smoke. Tracy and Natalie and I take turns standing outside on a tree stump, pretending to give the sermon. We jab our fingers in the air and raise our hands up and offer each other blessings. By the time it's dark, everyone is busy with the Peace-Be-With-You hug. We hug guys and girls. We hug Pastor Rick and the student priest and Dirk and Dirk's wife. We stay up late singing hymns to the strum of Pastor Rick's guitar. We fall asleep smiling and wake up in bunk beds that smell like old cheese. Dirk wakes us up with a trumpet call that sounds like a rooster.

Processions, etc.

- *At all times, don't be too slow or too fast*
- *Check out the last hymn at the end of the service and decide when it might be best to leave*

On Saturday night at Beauty Lake Bible Camp, Dirk's wife drives to town for more popcorn and marshmallows. Pastor Rick and the student priest lead the boys on a night hike. The rest of us drag our sleeping bags into the small chapel for the First Annual Sleepover. Tracy brings pop and chips and bug spray. Natalie borrows the camp nurse's tape machine and plays "Mandy" over and over again. Her cousin brings comic books. And Dirk brings a knapsack of girl magazines. He brings so many, we don't even have to share. We move the chapel pews and sit in a circle on the floor. When we're done with one

Playboy magazine, we pass it along to the next girl. And the next girl passes us back a *Penthouse.* Tracy says, "Woo, I'm getting a little hot under the collar," because she's in grade eight. Natalie starts pressing her knees together and pretending she's praying. Some girls are giggling. Later on, we play balloon soccer until someone knocks over a pop bottle and spills Dr. Pepper on the altar cloth and Dirk blames it on me.

I don't even drink Dr. Pepper, but I apologize to God in front of everyone just so Dirk will give me a thumbs-up. Maybe he feels bad about blaming me, because later on Dirk walks me out to the girl's shower house with his flashlight so I can brush my teeth and get ready for bed. I look at my eyes in the mirror and splash my face. I say my prayers. I flush the toilet a few times. I floss my teeth. When I finally come out in my pajamas, Dirk is still standing there, waiting for me. "Hey!" Dirk says, waving his flashlight at me. "Jesus wore pajamas just like yours!"

Snowball

Your parents are allowed. Your parents do it safe and snug in their own warm bed while the white dog lies on the floor, chewing ice from her paws. Your parents do it, and when they're done, they worry that you're not yet home.

You're busy with the contraceptive foam at twenty below from an aerosol can your boyfriend warms in his armpit as best he can and drills you full of. A cool kind of foreplay, a snowball at recess, so you'll ride him, ride him like a sleigh with horse bells down the steep banks of the North Saskatchewan River. And you do.

Like this, just to stay warm, with your jeans jammed down stiff around your knees, moon boots knocking, downfill pulled up over your wind-whipped tits. You make him wave delirious angels in the snow, next to that creaking river, warming him up with a mouth full of steam. And when he flips you over and drives you forward like sled dog, oh yeah, you know that he'll come soon, too soon, and that you won't come until you're eighteen, at least.

"It's man against nature out here," he tells you, dabbing with his glove at a frozen bit of spunk. "Man against nature, baby."

Let Not Your Hearts be Troubled

All the Child I Ever Had Sleeps Yonder

T*he dying d*ay begins like every other day at the Whitman Mission, with ice water on Matilda's face and prayers to little Lord Jesus, and the wailing outside for the Indian babies dead in the night. The Mission stinks of measles and the onions rotting in the field. All Matilda has left is her sister's soft, warm back against her in bed and the taste of her sour thumb and the noises in her head. Outside, Dr. Whitman cries out and the Walla Walla Creek sips at the dusty ground. Far away on the prairie, her mama is gently snoring. Her mama sewn up in a white sheet and covered in rocks, so coyotes won't choke on her bones. *Sweet Jesus, sweet Jesus, oh please. Sweet Jesus, please.*

Her mama once held everything up to the light. Back in Platte County, her clean white hands stitched tiny bursts of colour. Naomi Sager did fine, fancy work in netting and embroidery. Her Missouri neighbours always knocked at her door, seeking advice. They'd tip their hats and ask Naomi to open the slim, tattered envelopes kept safe in their coats. She'd read out the tears and longings of family far away. She'd sit down and write a reply. On the Sabbath, Naomi gathered up her children for Sunday school. When there was a funeral, she dressed them in black and brought them to pay respects, whether the Sagers knew the dead man or not. The neighbours looked up to Naomi Sager as an oracle. They believed she could see the future with the light in her eyes.

Naomi saw herself standing on the riverbank at Independence. Waiting for the wagons and the cattle to cross the Missouri River first. The brown water licking at her ankles and her legs and sucking her under. She was bawling, as loud as the calves. Crying, "Henry! Henry, I won't live to see this through!"

*

In the night, Henry Sager lay on his wife with her neat mouth and soft gown. He wanted to chew her, to rouse this clergyman's daughter, to hang her from the stirrups off the back of his saddle. He wanted to whip her with his quirt and beat the Baptist out of Naomi and shout, "Giddyap!" Instead, he rolled off of her and stared into the dark of their bedroom. He was choking. He couldn't breathe there in Platte County. He wanted his wife to feel his desperation, to feel the same fear as he tightened his hands around her neck.

In those days, if there was a death at hand, Henry made the coffin. If anyone needed a horseshoe or a spinning wheel or a loom, he was the man to make it. Henry Sager made everything in common use but a saddle. He could make one of those, too, if he set about it. But he felt defeated by neighbours and fences and the children tumbling out. Elizabeth was born the Year of the Panic and then John and Francis and Catherine and Matilda and Louise and they were not even the beginning or the end of the offspring.

Trumpener

Those were the days when the Sager family had a house with a window and a door. The yard was like parchment and the children would write in the dust with sticks and Matilda would hike her dress up and squat to erase it with her water. She milked cows and chased chickens and she was never alone. But her papa had a fever. He heard voices that said, "That-a-way! That-a-way!" He believed the tips of the stars were pointing west. If his wife stood in his way, he vowed to strike her down. When she begged him to stay, he swore he'd leave them all behind. Naomi put on her shoes and closed the door and followed behind him.

That is how they set out for Oregon, with a wagon as thin as a casket, and Matilda's mama bawling on the riverbank. Her papa was beating at their cattle. The cows had seen the far shore and turned back, stampeding for home. They leaked their milk into the water. Calves turned belly up and floated away down-river. Matilda's mama clutched at her children and her tight, round belly. Matilda's papa could make anything, it was true. But he couldn't make this right.

With a wagon so narrow, they walk alongside. They leave their oak dresser on a hillside and don't look back. Matilda makes up rhyming songs for the sound of the wind or the way the dust tastes or the roll of the wheel. There's no difference between outside and in, nothing between the earth and her skin. Her papa tells her Virginia and the Ohio Valley and Missouri were never home. They were just a resting place. Now there's no rest. Her papa carries the gun and says they're bound for the Promised Land.

Moving, moving, the wheels of the wagon carrying her mama, tossing her and rocking her and letting go of home.

Burnt River, Powder River, Grande Ronde. A lurch. A lurch. A lurch. Clouds of clinging dust. The wheels move Naomi forward, so she can't stay in one place at all. The whole earth swallowed up in her dry mouth. And one morning, Naomi's panting like the oxen, her hips bumping along with the wagon, legs split up to the sky, and then there are nine Sager children. The new baby is Henrietta, laid out on a rough sheet of prairie and rocked to sleep.

Women shiver about the Sioux and the Pawnee and cry in fear. As the sun goes down, the men march around the wagons with their rifles. They call themselves a militia and make Henry Sager their Colonel. One man beats a drum that wakes the new baby. The moon rises. Naomi dreams their new home has tough, sharp grass and a heart of stone. She wakes up soaked in milk. The baby's head smells sweet.

The wagons roll. One night, the bedclothes catch fire. The next week, Henry's militia fires at two pioneer girls out getting wood. Later, they stake a man out in the sun all day for bothering children in the camp. One hot month, the Nemaha River rises and runs through the tents and floods the ground. Climbing up to higher ground, the oxen slip and drag two wagons down behind them. In the mountains, a wagon catches Catherine Sager's dress and crushes her leg in a wheel. A herd of buffalo shakes the earth and fills the valley with big woolen heads.

Henry takes sick with camp fever and then his wife does too. Catherine lies between them in the thin wagon with her splinted leg and her papa says, "Poor girl. What will become of you when your father dies?" And those are the last words he ever speaks. He dies at Green River.

Trumpener

John Sager takes his father's gun and rides ahead for help. His brother, Francis, hangs a sheet over the wagon to keep out the dust. Inside, where their mama lies frantic with fever, it smells like rotten stew. Naomi begs her son to keep the girls together. She calls to her husband as if he were still alive. "Oh Henry. If you only knew how we suffered."

They sew Naomi into a sheet. She looks hot and unhappy and doesn't answer when Matilda calls out to her and cries. Francis and Louise help dig a hole at Pilgrim Springs and cover it with willow. They leave their mother to her long sleep. The wagons roll away. Inside, Catherine rocks her baby sister. Mothers share the baby at their breasts. A militia party is sent ahead to look for John and ask for flour and to see if the Whitmans will take in the Sager orphans at the Mission.

Mrs. Whitman's own baby has already drowned in the Walla Walla Creek. "All the child I had lies yonder," she tells them. She sends back her answer. She will keep the Sager baby, but she does not care for the older boys and girls.

But exceptions are made in the Promised Land. There are prayers and pleas. Dr. Whitman lets all the Sagers stay, Elizabeth and Catherine and John and Frank and Matilda and Louise and baby Henrietta. He is a Christian man in a lonesome place shut away back in the hills, where the Cayuse babies are dying every day.

Matilda and her sisters are put to work. They ring bells in the corn to keep the crows away. Wolves hide in the sharp rye grass where Matilda and her sisters walk through without shoes. Snakes slither in the wild parsnip. Mrs. Whitman teaches them their night prayers: *Let Not Your Hearts be Troubled.*

On the dying day, Matilda wakes up to gunshots and the rattle of dried berries as Cayuse warriors empty the pantry. Downstairs, Mrs. Whitman shouts, "I am wounded, hold me tight!" Matilda has nothing but her prayers and the warm back of her sister to protect her.

Zap Valley

Dirty Sox

I*t was* the winter you slept with Manny, who called his penis lumber. Or maybe he called it timber. Was it kindling?

You were studying history at a college in a small town that smelled like oatmeal. Damp snow fell outside like cotton soaked in milk, muffling the dark streets. Manny's roommate was out of town, down south. You stamped your boots and climbed the stairs of Manny's old apartment building. The radiators hissed and Manny opened the door and bent down to kiss the snow off your forehead. And you leaned against him and smelled beets and cauliflower, and the rough wool from his sweater scratched your cheek.

There were already signs that Manny would become handsome and far too cool for you. But in those days, he still had big glasses and alarmed eyes and slicked back hair and he was way behind on all his essays. He suffered a lot. He brooded in silence. He tried to take up smoking. He had a roommate named McCale, with smooth skin and radiant teeth, who used to make him laugh. But McCale was away that winter, doing a Semester Abroad in South America, and so Manny was lonely and he liked having you stay over.

Once in the middle of the night, Manny rolled onto the floor and lay there moaning, "Tell me what to do. Just tell me what to do!" You tried to help him. You helped him write outlines for his essays. You broke down *"Great Expectations: Images of Imprisonment and Release"* onto index cards. You broke the story down into small pieces and lay the index cards end to end along the hall from his bedroom to the kitchen, and then taped them together into a very tall puzzle. You typed the essay for him on a Selectric typewriter that whirred at the end of every line. Later, you took mushrooms and lay down on his futon and had an orgasm out your armpit.

When you weren't busy typing, you spent a lot of time lying on Manny's futon, sleeping off your antidepressants. Earlier that autumn, you'd suffered a lot. You walked through bushes, so that people standing at the bus stop wouldn't see you. With a pink plastic Lady Gillette razor, you tried to slash the top of your wrist — the side with no veins. It only made stinging little cuts that didn't bleed at all. Your academic advisor offered you a Valium from her purse. She offered you an extension on your essays.

You went to the hospital and cried when they asked your name. In those days, they didn't have gentle, happy pills with names like Love-Ox. Instead, they sent you home with an ugly drug that filled your mouth with cotton. Your ears echoed. You slept all the time and you woke up frightened and then the drugs dragged you back down into sleep again. You wrote poems in your diary like:

closed dark curtains
mourners dressed in black nothing
slip by
slip by the undertow

The doctor warned you that the day you stopped taking your antidepressant pills, you'd dream you were dead. "Wow!" said Manny. "Wow."

When Manny was young, his father used to punish the kids in weird ways. He'd make them pick crumbs and fluff out of the carpet. "Pick up the bits, pick up the bits!" his father would shout, kicking at them with his corduroy slippers. All the kids down on their hands and knees, digging for bits of dirt. Manny tells you there was a time he felt so bad, he wanted to be hit by oncoming cars. "But just gently, right?" he told you.

You were both envious of McCale, sending happy postcards home from Latin America. He was buying woolen socks and indigenous knapsacks in the markets. He was sleeping outside after a 7.2 earthquake. He was hanging out with the shoeshine boys. You wondered if you would always get left out. You tried not to think about it, but you were envious of carefree kids studying textile cooperatives in Latin America. You were jealous of the packs of students drinking cheap pitchers of draft in the basement of The Sow's Ear, the ones staying out all night and turning up at Hannah Ann's Café for the breakfast special, laughing and sweating beer and ordering extra toast before heading home to bed.

You were more likely to spend your nights haunting the campus library, a huge building full of untouched books and quiet floors. Sometimes it seemed you were the only one there, hunting down books on the historiography of Nazi postage stamps. The library hummed and the wind off the river rattled the windows. Across the bridge, the student dorms were buried in snow, and you wrote your notes on small index cards, and waited for the thaw.

It was the end of winter when McCale flew home. He climbed the creaking stairs to the old apartment and sat down grinning on the hallway floor. He smelled funny. He opened his backpack. You watched as McCale unpacked his dirty socks and showed you the cocaine he'd stashed inside to fool the drug dogs and pay his tuition. You knew nothing about weight or heft or ounces or grams. But the drugs were all gone in no time, and McCale forgot to ask for any money and he didn't make a cent. You still remember the blue patterned china plate from Manny's kitchen coming up and up toward your face, morning and afternoon. You snorted cocaine through dollar bills and rubbed the powder on your gums. You felt jumpy and awake and alive. Years later, you can still bring back the taste it left in Manny's mouth. It was sweet and sharp, like warm blood with a dash of snot.

The day before McCale flew home, you and Manny were enjoying breakfast at Hannah Ann's Café: eggs and bacon and rye toast and home fries dipped in a special mayonnaise dressing and coffee with cream and Nanaimo bars. And you said to Manny, "Your love is making me fat," and you both laughed. And then you walked back to his place along the train tracks, feeling sluggish and sleepy and vowing to finish your essays. And the snow was just starting to melt and you kicked at the slush with your boots.

Where It Hurts

Once, I looked out the streetcar window and saw a man flying through the air. He landed on Queen Street, amidst coins from his pocket and his right shoe, which had come off in flight. I was late for work.

I comforted him. I crouched behind him on the road and held his neck stiff, my thumbs along the blade of his jaw, as he called out "Broken! Broken!" to the crowd that had gathered.

I told him that everything was going to be fine, although it was only a guess. I asked him his name. I asked him where it hurt. I said, "Tell me where it hurts," calm as anything.

The driver who had hit him was chasing dimes along the road. She held them out to us like an apology, "Here." She was breathing hard. "Don't," I told her. "Just stop."

Moments passed, or hours. A policeman leaned out of his cruiser window to say sorry, he was on his way to a breakfast meeting, but he'd call in the accident.

I turned towards the streetcar, its back door still wide open, and called out for a jacket to cover this man on the road. A beautiful fellow came forward and squatted down in front of us, holding a paperback novel in his hands. He offered to help, but he never let go of the book. I can still remember the cover.

Me, squatting on the roadway with the broken man's hair in my hands, and everything all around us stopped.

Later on, after they'd taken him away by ambulance, police drew chalk marks around where his body had landed. They asked me, "About here?"

"About there," I agreed.

The beautiful man with the novel came and sat with me on the sidewalk. I was late for work. I was shaking. He put down his book and took my face in his hands. The streetcar rolled past as if everything was okay again and so I kissed him. And he kissed back, first my top lip and then the bottom, and the first policeman came by, full of breakfast, and said, "Sorry it took so long," and covered us with a blanket. And even while we kissed under the blanket, I was shaking, knowing that sometime soon, he was going to put my face down and pick up his book again.

Emergencies

Warm in my Hands

I carry their blood to the lab, still warm in my hands.

I carry their blood upstairs. Past the ancient operating room elevator, where the uniformed attendant slides open the grill door with his white gloves, as if All Saints Hospital is a Parisian apartment block or an upscale Inferno. Carry it past the dog show put on for in-patients, cocker spaniels parading between the blood bank and the micro lab.

It's one of my duties. The nurses call for me on the inter-com—"Blood to lab in major, blood to lab"—and I go and get it, blood and urine and black sputum in a sandwich bag.

I Am Mistaken

In Emergency, new people keep swinging through the doors all night long, and they hurt and they hurt and they hurt. I sit beside them in the dark. I want to offer them relief before they've even asked.

"You can't save them all," the charge nurse tells me cheer-
fully, and sends me off with a box of Kleenex for the family of
Bed 3, a construction accident.

Other things I do in Emergency: on request, I change the
waiting room TV to the *Miss America Pageant*. I call the cat-
minder for a patient going in for gall bladder surgery. I keep
an eye on Honey, drawing class valentines alone in the waiting
room while her father bleeds inside, pooling lakes of bruises
below his eyes. I am mistaken both for a nurse and an angel.

Your Father Was Lying

One nurse always asks nicely for things. She calls me over and
asks, "Can you bring down a duck lamp from ICU? Please and
thank you." The Good Nurse wears an old-fashioned peaked
nurse's cap as if she's from another era. Her cap reminds you of
the paper napkin your mother once pinned to your head with
bobby pins before sending you outside with an aspirin and a
glass of water for your father.

Your father had a headache. He was lying on the green lawn
chair in the backyard, freshly mowed with unhappiness.

Your father took the glass of water and the aspirin and
reminded you that when he gets old, if he even makes it that far,
you are to finish him off. Then he hands you back the glass.

Names of the Tiny Bones

All Saints Hospital
A CENTURY OF CARING

Please explain why you wish to volunteer at
All Saints Hospital Emergency Department
and describe relevant experience, if any.

• *Because I enjoy helping others. It makes me feel good. It makes
me feel better.*

• *Because when I was on the Freedom Brigade in Aujano and
in love, they drove us straight from the fields to watch hernia
surgery at Hospital Juan Luis Molina. One minute I was
picking guavas with campesinos, sick with sweat and the wormy
fruit. The next, I stood at the window of the operating suite, the
surgeon waving out at me, and my lover behind, wrapping his
arms around me, the guava juice still slick on his hands.*

• *Because my Thursday nights are free (so far).*

• *Because I want to learn things that don't matter at all to
ideology, like which fridge to put the urine samples in, or how to
culture a bursa, or the names of the tiny bones of the feet.*

• *Because a Bavarian farmer fed my father's hand into a
threshing machine after the war and from the back seat of the car,
I watched that scar drive us across Canada.*

The One Who Lived

Long ago, your grandmother took a look at her three sons, the two who had died and the one who still lived, and decided she could not save any of them. So the war raised your father, and there was no one left to raise you. Your father could not reconcile your small needs with the dead airmen who'd hung from the trees in his yard, or the soldiers intent on his mother's meat, hidden away in the attic.

Troubled by Ghosts

The Good Nurse shares her chocolate almonds with me. She says she's troubled by ghosts. They haunt her. When she walks by the Neuro ICU on her way to dinner, hairs rise up on the back of her neck. When she passes the chapel, she feels a short, hot breeze. She hears sensible shoes tapping down the long, winding corridors, following the beep of the CAT scan.

"It's the nuns," she tells me. "All Saints' old nursing nuns. Dead almost a century, those old girls, but they're still not done." I shake my head. "That's a long shift," I say, and we laugh. I reach for another chocolate almond. "Listen," the Good Nurse says. She hears the rustle of their habits.

Putting out Fire

Your father is a child. He has already woken his parents and led them in their nightshirts down the dark stairs of the old apartment block on Edelstraße, his palm dragging against the

emergencies

Trumpener

wood railing, his bare feet lit up every few steps, into the bomb shelter.

Now he is back upstairs with a pail of water, thinking about his dream. The apartment block was like a long, tall dollhouse you could look right into. He dreamt that he could see his neighbours falling through the building, top to bottom. When he woke up, he wished that the people falling were his parents, who gave his sugar ration to the dinner guests.

Tonight his parents are in the shelter while bombs fall, floor to floor, through the building. He has to chase the bombs, clunking down the stairs in his pajamas with the moon outside, putting out fires with his bucket of water. It's one of his duties.

Other things he will do in time: He'll give directions to the Russian tanks rolling into Berlin. He'll learn the names of all the stops on the Trans-Siberian Railway. He'll travel without food for days on the backs of trains searching for his mother. In Canada, he'll see a psychologist who will listen and say nothing.

Not a Seamstress

"Been walking here for days," she tells me, this dishevelled woman on the assessment bench, weeping in great gulps so loud that the triage nurse stays away, stays inside the office.

"Took weeks just to get here with the frostbite in my toes," she tells me. "Now can I see a fucking doctor and not a seamstress?"

Later, I bring sandwiches (at first, just two: ham and roast beef) to a hungry old man on a stretcher. He eats one after the other, dropping the wrappers on the floor. He insists again and again that I am starving him.

"But you haven't given me anything to eat!" he says. "I'm hungry!"

So I feed him everything in the patient fridge, including lemon pudding using a tongue depressor as a spoon.

These Things

These things come to Emergency:

- The woman who swallowed her cigarette days ago, but only now finds that the filter is beginning to bother her.

- A motorcycle accident bleeding out the bottom of his feet.

- The well-dressed, when their night out has gone really wrong, a heart attack or a massive allergic reaction. A nurse leads them itching and gasping into Major. She lays them down on a bed and leans close to feel their breath on her cheek. They struggle against their swollen tongues for breath. They wonder who would put walnuts in a breast of chicken and why.

- A pudgy man with wispy blonde hair, complaining that he's being kept in sexual bondage. "They think I'm a big man," he sobs, "but I'm just a little baby girl." And who am I to say?

Death Registration

There's a sullen young guy I always see, coming in and out of Emergency with his arms full of files. One night, I follow him onto the elevator.

"What are you?" I finally ask.

"Death registration clerk," he says, and gets out on 3.

The Worst of It

Sometimes things are so dead that the nurses relax to the point of bitterness. They retreat to make Christmas crafts from yarn and latex on the tightly made empty beds in Major, and I tear hundreds of lab order labels. I send the ward aide for coffee so that I can tidy the waiting room. And when everything is still quiet, and I've mopped up spills of Orange Crush and tidied the STD pamphlet rack, the receptionist hands over Trauma Reports. It's a thin, black, dollar-store binder, full of 401 highway wreckage and jumps from the viaduct.

Trauma is severe, the triage nurse tells me, a life-threatening injury, usually to more than one organ system. Trauma is the worst of it.

After trauma, the emerg doctors write up a report, an odd little story in the passive voice, and put it in the binder. Here's one about the man who shot himself in the head with a nail gun. *Unlike a bullet, the nail moves through the brain too slowly to sterilize its trajectory, and must be removed.*

In a strange, sad way, it gave me hope: all that we can suffer and still survive.

Getting Close

These things come to Emergency:

   •A cop on a stretcher, spitting bullet blood into a cup on his chest, his head wrapped in a towel as if he's suffering an old-fashioned earache.

   •Your father, whose hand was fed into a threshing machine just after the war. "You can't imagine how it felt," your father used to say, bedtime story over, as he turned off the light. And you would lie there in the dark with your tight heart, exhausted by a child's effort to keep her father alive.

You could never imagine how he felt. Even now, you can't. But you feel you're getting close.

emergencies

Trumpener

Ringside

The neighbours almost never say anything to you, or to each other, but strange things are starting to happen. It's a rainy night and some policemen down below the building are waving their flashlight beams against the ground. The neighbour lady from 604 leans around the balcony divide and says, "I suppose they're down there catching worms."

Then she goes back inside.

Things like this bring you out onto the balcony: sirens and shrill screams and the need for fresh air. There's plenty of all of these after eleven at night. "Ringside seats," the hardware clerk told you when you bought the patio chair.

Last year, a guy pushed his date out of the car as they were speeding down your street, and she lay there on the road with a broken neck. You kept having dreams about the angel brace they screwed into her skull.

The other week you saw—no lie—two ambulance attendants swinging billy clubs at a body on the sidewalk.

Used to be all you had to worry about was the bus running over your toes. Now you do as they say—hurry on along inside. But even from up here, high up in a row of silent, blinded buildings, you can't help but see what's going on. You're a witness, tired and alarmed and angry that the night is keeping you awake again.

Dinner yesterday was simple. You put in the chicken to bake and set the timer. You washed some green beans and snapped off their tails. You decided against a salad. You thought you'd take a moment to check outside.

Rain was coming down in sharp, cruel slaps. Across the street, some kids were splashing around in a fridge laid on its back and abandoned on the lawn. It made you think of open caskets, and then the timer went off, a sharp drilling noise, and you went back inside to steam the beans.

On TV, being interviewed, was a criminal type with mist in his eyes, crying because he was fed up with living in jail. He was explaining why he wanted to die in the electric chair. The interviewer had eyebrows that seemed amused.

There was knocking at your door. Your building superintendent was there to tell you about the girl, the little girl who was missing, just disappeared. She was playing outside, down there, and then she wasn't.

The police are searching all around for her, crossing off whole blocks on colour-coded grid charts as they go. The police are standing here in the apartment hallway now, like large wet bats dripping rain on the carpet. They're rapping their knuckles against all the closed wooden doors stretching down the hall. You ask them in.

There's one thing you can't forget, the part of their search for a girl that's gone, and that is how they check inside your oven. Just this: the oven door opening and then slamming shut and nothing inside, only a chicken.

Trumpener

Push!

I*'m late* for pre-natal class. I see my man, Hamish, already on his mat, rolling from buttock to buttock, stretching out his big legs and flashing his bare toes. At the front stands another man, Mike, our pre-natal teacher. This is the kind of thing that happens in small towns, where a few good people have to spread themselves too thin. I've heard our teacher is the kind of man who doesn't mind baby spit or cunnilingus. I've heard he bones up for class with the diagrams in his daughter's tampon box. The kind of man who shouts "Push!" with a smile.

Our teacher waves me to the front of the room and brandishes a Q-tip.

"Swab time!" Mike says with a cheerful face. "Just pop it in your ear and swirl!"

I don't know if this is punishment for arriving late or preparation for cleaning our newborn's ears. But others are obviously in the know. A big-bellied woman waves her hand in the air. "Excuse me, excuse me! Nothing smaller than your elbow in your ear, please!"

Here I am, obediently swirling away, and the teacher claps

his hand and says, "Excellent!" But I don't know if he's praising me or her. It's the kind of mistake I seem to make too often.

Hamish never wanted kids. I begged to bear his dark-eyed, stout little snakes, but he said no one ever asked if they wanted to be born. "No one asked me," he sneered in bed, lifting my leg and flipping me over on his grandmother's quilt.

So my lap is still empty. Standing at the front of this pre-natal class feels like the time I ended up in the wrong line during Frosh Week registration and got a TB test and a spot of blood on my arm instead of a professor's permission to take Film Studies. The pre-natal teacher is saying, "Elbow! Exactly. Right. Good. And don't let your newborn fiddle with Cheerios, either."

Hamish says not everyone is meant to be a mother and so he never let his soldiers fly. Never, until he knocked up that skinny Argentinian girl who works down the street. Juanita tottered over on her red high heels to bang on our door and ask for my help. She called me Auntie. She said, "Por favor, Tia," and wept on our doorstep. The mascara ran down her face.

So I put down my Q-tip and go over to help her and Hamish on their pre-natal mat. Hamish is stroking Juanita's fat little tummy. The teacher starts passing out speculums that look like giant eyelash curlers.

Needle Exchange

We're on holiday, and a man is sticking drugs into his arm. His back is to the ocean and he looks for a vein and he sticks the needle in his arm and then he howls. He's quiet, and then he howls again. My daughter is cutting the sand with seashells and the howling hurts her ears. I want to tell her it's a whale in distress, but it sounds more like a monster or a man eating a bowl of jagged glass, spoonful after spoonful. And it takes awhile, long enough for three slim yellow kayaks to slide by us on the lip of the sea. We are relaxing. And until the man on the beach started howling, the most distressing thing we'd faced so far was the lifeguard at Second Beach Pool yelling, "Hey! No sliding headfirst down the Seal Slide!"

My daughter's watched her father slide headfirst before. He's a diabolic diabetic. When things get rough, he swallows a fistful of brown sugar or sticks needles into the tough, bruised skin above his hip. Sometimes, my daughter tries to do the same thing. This morning, she stuck herself with the sharp end of the small paper parasol that was decorating the mango pudding at Dim Sum at the Pink Pearl Restaurant on

East Hastings. We ate lions' heads and shrimp dumplings and mango pudding and then my daughter took the paper parasol from the pudding and lifted up her shirt and stuck the sharp end of the tiny umbrella into the soft skin of her belly. On our way back to the beach, I raced her past Alibi Pizza. We ran past a man in a fez who was carrying a steaming kettle in his hands. A tourist stopped us to ask if this was a street fair, because everyone in the Downtown Eastside was selling something out on the sidewalk.

My daughter has seen her father forget his own name before. She's watched as I tried to pour orange juice and sugar into his mouth. And I swore that time, because the juice just pooled in the hollow below his neck and left little puddles in the sheets and I didn't know what to do. I called for help. The volunteer firemen got there first and they clomped in with their big boots and stood shyly around the bed, shifting their weight from foot to foot. One of them lifted my daughter into his arms while I stormed the pantry. I tore open a can of lychees and I fed it to my man with a baby spoon. And by the time the ambulance raced up, I was already saving him with fruit and syrup and sweetness in a spoon.

Trumpener

Satan's House

Keith hands me a tea bag. It's wet and warm and there's a tiny twig sticking out of it.

He says, "This is my testicle."

He says, "Keep it for me, will ya?"

The tea bag bleeds onto my hand. I say, "Keith, man, it's time to go."

And he says, "I mean it. My lady's in hospital. I gotta sleep at Satan's House tonight. They'll boil my bag up for dinner and then I'm done for. You gotta keep it safe."

*

Butchie's been swabbing down the tables with a rag from the kitchen, heaving up chairs, emptying ashtrays, shouting, "Who left their dirty Mr. Noodle dishes out here? Come on, people, who's going to wash up!?" and no one even turns to look, too busy packing up their blankets and shit into BiWay bags. A squeegie guy's already banging on the door, begging to run his soaking socks through the dryer once, just once, "S'il vous plait, come on, mon chum." Leisha asking to borrow a loonie or two from me, "Pay you back tomorrow, got no streetcar ticket to get to Out of the

Cold and eat some stew."

Butchie's shouting, "Quit dawdling, five o'clock. Let's go, folks!" And that's when this guy, Keith, hands me his tea bag, and I'm holding it and it's leaching brown stuff onto my palm and I'm thinking of the henna designs they drew on Mina's hands before she got married.

And then we're closed and Butchie's locking the Good Shepherd's Day Shelter door and everyone's heading out into the rain.

Some of the guys heading out the door are nasty. Angrier than my father, even. Sit here and simmer. You might be playing euchre and someone will freak out and be like: "I said jail rules, ya dumb fuck!"

One time, this friend of Riley's waved his pool cue at my head, after I told them to let the women play. I hid in the staff office and bawled, sitting on the floor below the windows so no one would see me.

But Keith's usually pretty good.

I remember a long time ago we watched this movie when we were kids in Sunday school. In the movie a clown was washing people's feet inside a circus tent. And all these people with dirty shoes were laughing and hee-hawing at the clown, until they finally turned on him and killed him. I felt sorry for that clown. I really did. He was just cleaning people's shoes with a brush. He never asked to be crucified.

That's kind of how I feel about it.

Last winter, this old guy came in with an old woman and they were both freezing. They needed coats. So I sent them down to the donations room in the basement. But they took a long time,

Trumpener

and when I went downstairs, they were in there fucking on a pile of dresses, donations from someone's dead grandmother. I had to kick them out, coats or no coats. The old man just shrugged at me. "We got nowhere else to get it on." He wasn't even mad.

Every evening, I head back home through their turf—"Hey, Riley, hey, where you sleeping?"— to my high-rise apartment. I have a big old empty bed and lots of square feet. I sit alone watching TV.

In the morning, I'm back here, mopping vomit off the front steps in the rain.

While I'm swabbing down the cement with bleach, the lady from the gallery across the street stands frowning at me from under her umbrella. I want to tell her that Jesus was a homeless baby, but I don't really have the energy, so I just mop.

*

"**K**eith trusts you with his balls?" asks Butchie, shaking his head and letting out a mouthful of smoke. "Oh, girl!"

It's the end-of-the-week staff meeting. Everyone sits and smokes and writes down the worst shit of the week in a black book we keep locked in the staff office. Tattletales.

> • *T broke leg; stitches on ankles and knees but hospital won't keep her and no $ for crutches; Butchie will check w/hospital social worker.*
>
> • *New woman (Cathy?) lost apt, staying with friends, may lose kids.*
>
> • *K gave Sheryl a tea bag and said was his "testicle".*

• R and N helping at reception; maybe doing crack deals on the phone? Yes: bar for two weeks. Mina will talk w/them.

*

Mina's the boss. She asks if I feel "okay" about Keith handing me something as if it's his testicle.

"Well, it's kinda gross," I say. "But I guess he's sleeping over at the men's hostel, at Saint Anne's Place. So he's just worried about his stuff getting ripped off. So, whatever. I could keep it for him. I don't mind. Or I could just brew him a new one when he comes back."

"Well," Mina says, blowing out smoke, "check it out with him. But please let him know it's not okay to be saying stuff like that to the staff."

The social work intern writes that down in the black book.

• Sheryl will check in with K about his tea bag and may offer to keep it safe.

Then the intern re-ties her ponytail.

*

After the staff meeting, we sometimes go drinking down the street. I don't really drink much, but some of the staff, the ones who've been here way too long, they pour it back until they sob about their own sorry lives. It's a bit much at the end of the day.

Once they've ordered another round of draft, the intern says she heard the street nurse say Keith had to sleep at Satan's House because of his operation.

Butchie says the operation and the infection are Keith's own damn fault for being such a slut. "How come none of us can get laid and Keith is always shacking up and slipping out to go fuck in the alley?"

Mina says that's bullshit. She says Keith was sleeping out all summer inside the urinals at Oak Park where he couldn't bathe so the infection couldn't drain and the whole thing never healed. She says Keith's testicle, swollen as big as a grapefruit, is now floating in a formaldehyde bath on the desk of some surgeon at the hospital downtown.

Butchie snickers and tells me I better get back to work and dig that tea bag out of the trash.

"I saw you toss it," he says.

"Whatever," I say. "You're on drugs."

*

Monday morning, I come in early to make 150 tuna sandwiches for the protest against homeless deaths. The intern shows up to help me, along with Keith and Riley and a guy with sores on his face, who falls asleep against the stove.

The intern puts the kettle on to boil.

Riley starts eating pickles from the jar.

And I open cans of tuna while Keith toasts and butters three hundred slices of white bread. He doesn't ask about his tea bag. He tells me his lady friend got fried in her sleep from a steam vent.

"Second degree," Keith tells me. "But it's healing pretty good."

He starts humming a country song.

Keith says when she gets out of hospital, he wants to give his lady a good night's sleep. He wants to buy her a comfortable bed.

"Right on," I tell him. "That's great."

A few weeks later, the cops pick up Keith for robbing a bank with her hairbrush.

Trumpener

The Coffin Maker

J ones *lives* beneath the coffin maker. Every night, late at night, right above his head, his neighbour is hammering thin nails into coffin lids. *Tunk. Tunk. Tunk. Tunk.* Jones lives right below all this industry, this never-ending noise, tossing and turning in his Murphy bed in his bachelor suite in the tallest apartment building on Queensway Avenue.

"You're a bachelor? Sweet!" is what the hookers tell Jones when he brings them back there for a roll in the hay, even though the elevator's busted and they can never sleep because of the hammering.

There's no intercom either. Every night, the coffin maker just jams open the building's front door with a crusty pizza box and his customers roll in to the lobby, looking for a place to wait, a place to rest and dream.

> *Coffins carved from dying pine!*
> *Boxes to lie down in!*
> *Caskets for all shapes and sizes!*
> *No order too small. Special snug fit for kids!*
> *Rush orders!*
> *Good prices! Group rates!*

Tunk. Tunk. Tunk. Tunk.

At night, when Jones takes the stairs down, two at a time, he can almost smell his neighbour's customers waiting down there in the lobby, lining up and lying down. Sometimes he has to wade through them just to get outside.

Tonight, there are so many people, they stretch right out the door. They're lounging on the patchy brown apartment grass or lying on charity sleeping bags, the thick, old-fashioned kind with pictures of hunters and ducks. Jones almost stumbles over the tiniest girl who's waiting in line. She can't be more than five. She's rocking back and forth on the lawn and crying.

Her Grandpoppa dropped her off earlier in her pajamas with feet. He said to her, "Serena, you better stay put or I'll smack you silly if you lose my place in line." He sped away fast in a taxi full of yellow smoke and never even asked if she needed to go pee. Her Grandpoppa hasn't been seen since. So Serena crawls up next to the only person who smiles at her, even though that woman has a bum leg and a boiled egg in her eye.

Jones tries to push his way through them, but the limping lady with the battered eye lurches up to him. She pokes him with a screwdriver and clutches at his arm for cash and Jones swings his fist right near her swollen face. He figures it's the only thing that will turn this lady sweet. And it does. Now she's saying *Please*. Now she wants to limp over to 7-11 with his hard-earned money to get some apple juice for the little girl who's sobbing and rocking. "Please," the woman says, putting down the screwdriver and grabbing the girl's hand. "She's up past her bedtime!" The limping lady tries to wipe the girl's tears on the bottom of Jones's T-shirt, but all the sobbing is hurting his head, so he takes off along Queensway to chase some tail.

Before he even hits city hall, he spies two scrawny girls who've just hitchhiked in from the res near the Skins Spillway, or at least that's what they tell them. He promises them cigarettes if they come up the hill. He marches them up Connaught Hill in their high heels and follows right behind, shining his key-ring flashlight beam at their skinny asses, cursing that they're too young to work it much.

From the top of the hill, his neighbour's hammering becomes just a dull thud in the distance. Jones sits for awhile in peace on a tree stump and the girls sit on a picnic table and pick mud off their shoes and smoke his smokes and dick around with his tiny flashlight and wait for their cell phones to ring. They wave his flashlight around and giggle about the trees up there that are covered in needle marks and oozing sap. Jones doesn't feel like laughing about the city's crazy pine bugs. He makes the girls kneel across the picnic table and slams into their sweaty backs, then puts out his cigarette. He comes up for air in the gentle stink of pulp.

Then he hears a loud noise, as though the coffin maker ran out of the building and followed them up the hill. As if his neighbour is taking his chainsaw to the pine trees. Jones drags the girls down quick under the picnic table, but the coffin maker is felling those goddamned dead trees so close by, Jones can't even hear the sounds the girls' lips make.

The girls get all scratchy and sour and starving. They cry that they're dying for daylight. Jones offers them chips and pop if they'll sleep on his floor. He follows them down the hill, back to Queensway.

The tiny girl is still outside his building, rocking herself and crying that she needs to go pee. And someone on the lawn yells, "Ain't that what playgrounds are for, sweetheart?" The limping lady is almost asleep in the grass, but she grabs at Jones's ankle as he walks past. She pulls herself up and tells Jones he better give her cash fast so she can get this little girl out of here and hide her away somewhere. The Skins Spillway girls laugh at that and keep walking, and the limping lady shouts after them, "At school, they cut my little tongue with scissors. At school, you whores!"

By the time Jones yanks the girls back up to his apartment, it sounds as if the coffin maker is close behind, dragging his dead wood up the fire stairs, one tree at a time, *thunk, thunk, thunk, thunk,* leaving dry, red needles behind him. And then he starts hammering again at his coffin lids.

Jones shouts up at him to shut up. He yells. He batters the ceiling with a broom handle. He grabs the Skins girls' shoes and cell phones and tosses them up at the ceiling like grenades. Nothing. *Tunk. Tunk. Tunk. Tunk.* The girls grab their stuff and slam the door behind them.

It's almost dawn. Jones calls the landlord. He calls the operator. He calls the cops. They tell Jones not to worry. They tell him his neighbour is chopping up meat on a cutting board for his breakfast stir-fry. They tell Jones the man must be nailing up family photos on the wall, preserving his memories of the whole damn clan. They tell Jones the man is weighing drugs on a rickety scale and smoking crack from a noisy pipe. They tell Jones his neighbour is nailing Jesus to the cross. They tell Jones, "Sir, just hang up and go back to bed." They call him *Sir.*

Jones heads upstairs ready to bust down the coffin maker's door and settle this once and for all. But the people ahead of him in line push him back. They say, "Wait your goddamn turn, buddy." So Jones heads down to the lobby, two steps at a time, crushing pine needles and kicking tree debris. He doesn't even get his chance to stand in line and wait his turn.

Outside on the lawn, the caretaker and a security guard and a mean-faced guard dog are driving everyone away. The caretaker charges at people with his mop and a bucket of bleach, shouting, "Buncha shit! You're all dirty shit!" And everyone is running away, even the little girl in her footed pajamas, and the mean dog is running right after them, and the sun's coming up.

Burning in Salango on Saturday Night

The night the villagers burned each other in effigy was the night Wolfgang fell in love. He woke up to the sound of cannon fire. He thought it was the beginning of a war and he went to investigate.

Wolfgang was staying at a tiny old hotel down the long dirt road from Salango. His bed was full of sand and seaweed. Sometimes, he'd sit on the empty beach and read his German Bible. Or he'd track down *Piquero de Patas Azules,* blue-footed boobies. The boobies would stamp their blue webbed feet and take flight whenever they saw him. But vultures never budged. If the birds took off on him, Wolfgang would go back to the beach near his hotel and read his paperback book about missionaries taken hostage by FARC guerillas and rescued by the love of God. He'd sit and read and scratch and pray until the sand flies drove him away.

Wolfgang read with thick glasses that magnified his eyes. His glasses helped him spot things far in the distance that aroused his curiosity. He'd wrap his swim towel around his neck and carry his Bible in a plastic bag and head off. One afternoon, he saw a flash on the horizon and followed it for an hour along the beach. The heat felt like pins and the sweat ran down his legs. He kept himself going with a song in his head: *Este huevo quiere sal. Este huevo quiere sal.* This egg wants salt! This egg wants salt!

A family from San Lorenzo was washing moray eels in low troughs beside a white wall. There was blood in the troughs. There was charcoal graffiti on the white walls: *Maria Magdelena! I love you and I miss you too much.* Wolfgang read it twice.

Then he turned his gaze to the daughters of the family from San Lorenzo. The girls had washed the eel blood from their hands and were now brushing each other's hair in front of a small shaving mirror. They all ignored Wolfgang.

Wolfgang was still young, but with his pale, thin wrists and thick glasses, he rarely gave off heat. He didn't inspire lust, even when he was sweltering and pulled his T-shirt above his nipples to keep cool. Still, he was the one who bragged that his love life didn't end with the Lord. He was emphatic and eloquent about that, even in a foreign language. "Oh, Dios, no chica!" he'd say. His Spanish got better the more whiskey he drank.

When Wolfgang was sober, his adoration was quieter, more worshipful. He liked to spend time around the young lady selling lemonade in front of the hut by the green bus bound for Misahualli. He liked to pour Evelynne's lemonade into his whiskey flask and flirt with her about God. When nobody was buying her lemonade, Evelynne played tin music by tapping her lemonade jar with a pair of forks. She played several songs, none of them very long.

Wolfgang wasn't really sure how things were going with Evelynne. When he talked to her sweetly or tried to read her the Bible, Evelynne usually looked down at her forks or went to sit in the shade. Her parents never told Wolfgang to go away, but they never invited him to join them for dinner, either.

Her father always sat at a card table near Evelynne, watching over six tan and brown pigs and a tapir with a fat penis, confined to a pen. No matter how hot it was, Evelynne's father always wore woolen knee socks. He tapped his feet in time to his daughter's fork music. At night, he washed his one white shirt with buttons and hung it on a line outside and that was the sign for Wolfgang to leave. Evelynne's mother was always busy roasting guinea pigs on skewers. She sold them to everyone who got off the bus, but tourists never wanted to buy them.

Tammy from Alaska was the first tourist ever to buy Evelynne's mother's *cui*. Tammy stepped off the bus in a track suit and wild hair. She looked around and swore and then she pointed at two skewers of meat from the grill and asked for some mustard. She had a beautiful, sloppy mole above her eye. Wolfgang offered to walk her to town to find condiments. He offered to carry Tammy's skewers if she'd carry his Bible.

Tammy had come to Salango to visit the shrine to La Virgen. La Virgen had saved the village from a volcanic eruption and rescued a peasant and his donkey as they slipped off a swinging bridge with their sugar cane. Tammy had also come to see the two-headed fetal pig fermenting in a glass jar on a shelf in the church museum. But first she wanted some goddamn mustard, and Wolfgang knew he would only disappoint her.

She seemed very angry, so Wolfgang offered Tammy his

whiskey flask instead. She handed back his Bible and poured some whiskey on her skewers and started to relax. They sat together on the church steps. Between bites, she told Wolfgang that her friends in Alaska always died in the winter when the ground was frozen. She said they always had to keep her friends' bodies frozen in freezers until the spring. Then there would be weeks of funerals, almost like spring weddings. Wolfgang wanted to ask how many of her friends had died and why they were killed, but instead he told her, "Spring without joy! Suffering without insight. The dead you can't bury." Tammy thought it was brilliant. She pulled off Wolfgang's glasses and kissed him. And Wolfgang whooped and said, "God has mercy! You see!" And Tammy licked her greasy fingers.

Wolfgang thought he was in Heaven. But after Tammy saw the fetal pig and the virgin and watched people feeding fat red grapes to monkeys hanging from the trees, she got on the bus again and waved goodbye. Evelynne's father said there was no lemonade left. Wolfgang went back to his hotel to fall asleep alone.

He woke up to the sound of cannons in the distance. A big boom and then a whistle and shells falling, round and heavy like coconuts or fire bombs. He started to pray, but thought better of it. He got dressed and walked to Salango in the dark, talking to God the whole way.

In Salango, people were sitting on low wooden planks just below the cemetery. They were drinking cane alcohol, offering it around like communion wine, and dancing, catching their heels in the dirt. Children were launching rockets on the dark side of the lot. The toffee vendor from the church square was wearing a dog mask and pretended to bark and whine and howl at

Wolfgang, even though they'd never really met before.

It didn't take long before Wolfgang was wearing the dog-mask and dancing a tip-tapping, hip-jumping salsa with Rodrigo's cousin. They were tipsy with cane alcohol and whiskey. Wolfgang had to put down his dance partner and his whiskey flask long enough to help carry the drunken husband of some woman named Benita to where her husband had to flag down the bus for his two weeks on at the oil rigs in Coca.

And Wolfgang shouted out to the night sky:

Römer. Kapital 11: So sage ich nun. Hat denn Gott sein Volk verstossen? Das sei ferne.

No one at the party in Salango could understand God's German, but it didn't matter. Rodrigo's cousin, Gloria, was pulling Wolfgang close for a silly, frantic two-step. At midnight, people started burning huge, stuffed puppets of some of the neighbours and the heat was intense. Gloria's face was alive in the dancing flames. Wolfgang asked her, "How does it feel, to watch yourself burn?" And she turned to him and that's all it took.

They walked hand in hand past the burned effigy bodies and the child swinging a rope of burning sparks over the charcoal. Further on, a sliver of moon lit up two white cows, still as ghosts in the middle of the road, and Gloria leaned in to his arm and murmured. Wolfgang hugged her and stood still a moment. He told her when he was little, the mayor of his village climbed to the top of their mountain and set a huge log on fire and pushed it over the cliff. The children all sat at the bottom and waited for the heat and rolling flames to scare away the devil. They hugged again.

All night, Gloria and Wolfgang sat together on the beach. She buried his feet in the sand. She let him nibble the tip of her thumb until he was all done. Wolfgang lay on the sand and started singing in a low, sweet voice:

> *When I fall down on my knees*
> *with my face to the rising sun*
> *oh, Lord, have mercy on me.*

He asked Gloria, "Have you ever seen pilgrims? Old women in stiff shoes with black heels? Hoping? Seeking?"

He was beautiful to listen to. Gloria sighed and reached for him. Their breath was still sour with whiskey. She said she wanted everything to be clear between them. She wanted to explain why her neighbours wanted to burn her down to ashes. She wanted to tell Wolfgang everything about Agado.

She told him Agado used to run to meet her, just so he would be slippery with sweat. He'd wait for her, lying naked on the floor of the dark schoolhouse until she slipped inside. Agado was dark and fat and strong. He mixed concrete: two sand, two gravel, one water, his pickaxe back and forth and back and forth. He'd pull open the one button of her white shorts. She'd take off her shirt and sink right onto him. Moths banged at the window screens and the jungle moaned outside. Mosquitoes bit at them, driving their desire.

One night, they heard the slap of feet and then a woman crying outside, knocking on the schoolhouse door. "Agado, Agado!" she cried, the tight wind of her longing. Gloria pushed herself up on Agado's chest to listen. Then she let herself down again and covered her mouth with his body. Agado ignored the crying outside and the insects dragging jagged saws across the leaves.

He moved inside of her. Then he took himself all the way out again and lay still. "Agado! Agado!" came again from outside. And that was their last time together.

The last time, except for the night Agado slipped into Gloria's room in the dark and crawled under the mosquito net with her. She used to feel safe under that net, she told Wolfgang, safe and protected. It was like a shroud or a burn bandage or a second set of looser, purer skin. All night, she and Agado lay underneath, listening to the toad croak in the toilet and the ceiling fan breathe above them.

On the beach, Gloria and Wolfgang slapped at the mosquitoes and the sand flies. They drew circles in the sand and scratched each other's bites.

Skin Condition

Already you have suffered from the diarrhea the locals call *La Cienaga Grande*, the Big Swamp. Already you have survived the shootout in the bar. One minute, everyone was beautiful and dancing and the next, you were knocking down chairs and clawing at strangers to hide your face between their bodies. You closed your eyes and lay with your nose against the floor, smelling someone's shoe. The music stopped and the screaming stopped and then it was very still.

When it was all over, people picked themselves up off the floor and brushed themselves off. Someone said, "That was like musical chairs," and everyone started dancing again.

You and Joa took the first bus out. The bus climbed up into the hills. It rolled on into lowlands bitter with saltwater swamps. The bus was express. It stopped only once, for a bull with an infected penis being loaded onto a flatbed truck that had stalled across the road. It made you think of bruised peaches. It made you happy to see everything through a window. You watched mile after mile of trees drowning in the ocean tides.

Joa insisted on getting off the bus in a town so foul it stained your armpits black. He wanted you to see a woman now famous as a palm reader or a prophet or maybe even a poet. You told him you didn't believe in anything anymore. He took you anyway.

The woman was expecting you. She looked at the drought on your hands, the dead, angry skin and the savage wounds. "In your house," she said, "there is someone heavy and tricky." She asked Joa to translate. She advised you to clean your house with ammonia, sugar and sulfur. She prescribed a bath of nine different leaves. She said, "Your skin is not from God." She asked you to come back on Thursday or Friday for an exorcism.

Joa was satisfied. You followed him across the street to a cafe where the air was almost fresh. You settled your swampy stomach with tea. Joa ate a plate of armadillo and smelled suspicious for days.

Tiny Crab

At *dusk*, an old man with a metal tank strapped to his back shuffled through the resort. He wandered by the restaurant table where you sat with Libby, spraying a chemical fog from his hose. His efforts made Libby choke. And they were too late for you. You'd had to lie down on a metal gurney while a cheerful nurse tied your dress above your legs and poured alcohol down your shins. She snipped at your infected mosquito bites with sterilized scissors and hummed.

That summer, Libby was losing her eyesight. After it got dark, you'd grab each other's arms to cross the beach back to your cabin. One night, a tiny crab was crushed in your cabana door. By morning, red ants from the soap dish on the side of the sink were eating the crab whole. Outside, the old man with the metal tank was now raking seaweed off the beach. He was erasing the footsteps of tourists who'd stood with their backs to the moon and watched a sea turtle drop her eggs down into a sandy hole. They had counted slowly, one to a hundred, in English. "Voyeurs," said Libby, who couldn't see much.

In daylight, you'd buy corn rubbed with lime and spices

from the sweating man on the seashore who shouted, "Choclos a tres cientos! Choclos a tres cientos!" He lifted the cobs off a charcoal grill and handed you two napkins. The corn stuck in your teeth. The sand rattled in your shoes. A white-haired man in long shorts called out, "How's that, now? Where can we get some of that cob?"

People on the beach were selling hair braids, corral earrings, gold coins, shrimp skewers, fishing trips and time-shares. One man in a hat asked if you wanted to buy some culture and you did. You and Libby followed him to a turquoise doorway and up three flights of stairs, where you found Frida Kahlo motionless on the floor, under a red sheet and bright lights. You were told to take off your shoes and sit on little pillows. There were so few of you there on the floor, you were shy about what came next. You were almost afraid to watch.

What came next was the steel rod from the Mexican street trolley crash that slid through Frida Kahlo's spine. Dancers in black masks waltzed in with a Frida doll so tall, you weren't sure who was the doll and who was the dancer. A tall skeleton jumped out to play the accordion. He played love songs to Frida, songs of adoration, with just the right tilt of his head. And you said to Libby, "That skeleton sure is spry with his squeeze box!" And you all clapped. And you remembered the sound that tiny crab made the night Libby couldn't see what was there and closed the door.

Short, Sad Night

Jalal's Birthday

On *your* twenty-fourth birthday, you and your best friend from jail got drunk on something rough in your highrise apartment on Lansdowne Avenue, where the trains ran past your living room window. The passengers heading home late to Oakville with their briefcases looked out the GO Train window and saw you stand up to recite poetry in Farsi. Over the train's mournful whistle, they could almost read your lips: *I have searched for you through dark graveyards.*

Never mind the distance between the train's smudged windows and your foreign verses. The commuters were as fascinated as I was. Then the train whooshed past and you stood up and vomited pickles on the carpet.

I stayed on the sofa, holding your small photo album in my lap, flipping through the pictures of your dead classmates and your *Maman-jan*, sitting alone in her village in northern Iran. I saw how you'd crossed over into Europe dressed all in white, as if you were a bride. Your arms were busy posing with all kinds of

Turks and Bulgarians, girls and older women wearing blue eye-shadow and knee-high nylons that cut into their plump legs

Come Inside and Be Happy

On our first night together, you took off all your clothes, except your underwear, and folded them neatly on the dresser, and then you lay on your back with your good hand folded behind your head and gazed up at the plaster swirls on the apartment ceiling, and smoked a cigarette. And time passed, but I was used to that.

Finally I whispered, "Jalal?"

And you answered, "Ateshenay hoshenol." Come inside and be happy. An invitation. But your voice was almost sad, and you didn't turn to look at me. Still, I joined you.

You had a hundred sweet names for me, for every part of me, even the parts that taste bitter.

That night, I dreamed the Nazis captured my father. They said they would set him free if I pulled off my own fingers. And so I did. It was winter. Steam came from the officers' mouths as they ordered me to remove my mittens. I popped my fingers out of their sockets, one by one, and tore them off my hand. It didn't even hurt.

Texas Hash

Your elevator smelled like Texas Hash and the hookers from Newfoundland who rented the studio suites. The elevator moved slowly. I was impatient. I was always so eager to see you.

Not just me. Everyone was always visiting you. Your best friend, gentle Abdi, who played chess in his track suit. Abdi's

Filipina girlfriend, who would whoop and giggle while they made love in the bathroom. Abdi's brother, Farid, whose brilliant green eyes shone from the opium. Farid's fat wife, Laila, who taught me to use glossy lipstick and got dizzy spells that rang in her ears.

You would put out a tablecloth on the living room floor and we would eat: white rice with a crust of potato and oil, and finely diced salads with lemon and mayonnaise, and chicken and pickles and cheap crystal fruit drinks from the discount grocery store below Dundas that's as big as an army barracks. I'd hear Farsi rhythms and sounds and forks waving, and I felt comfortably alone.

You'd cuddle me between your legs and talk and smoke in my hair and drink *chi* from a short glass and suck the sweetness from sugar cubes you gritted between your teeth. Sometimes you'd cook opium on the coffee table with a blowtorch and fill the room with hot, sweet smoke. Sometimes you'd toss down Tylenol 3s with codeine that Farid could get from the doctor near Christie Pitts.

They were good to have on hand. Once, Farid's wife, Laila, put their baby to sleep in your room and then sat down for tea as if everything was fine. But she dropped her glass and shrieked as if she couldn't breathe and crawled behind the sofa screaming until the neighbour next door banged on the wall with her boots and everyone whispered sweet words and stroked Laila's head, or what they could reach of it, until she came out of hiding.

Bike Chain

You were the tough one. The flat nose, the sharp bones, the firm, scarred hands that made me want to kiss you. You would come in at four in the morning after delivering pizza. Once, a gang of kids from Jane and Finch slashed the back of your head with a bike chain, trying to get your cash. And an old man in slippers had drawn out his penis in the elevator, while your hands were full of pizza. I would wake up with you on top of me and a flat box of Hawaiian Deluxe in the fridge, the cheese turning hard in the cold.

You were so goddamn beautiful I'd let you wake me up and tie me to the curtains and do me like that, with the moon beating down outside on the empty train tracks.

Kidneys

The night I woke up smelling rancid aftershave, the bitter lemon stink was from your kidneys, twirling on their stems. You said long ago, they'd been struck hard enough and long enough to keep them spinning for years.

I'd never heard you cry before.

I sped you down Dundas Street although I couldn't drive, steering between the shine of the streetlights on the streetcar tracks.

The lights in Emergency were blinding and you barely knew me. One nurse hated your name and jammed a thermometer up your ass. She asked you what was wrong in a booming voice, her lips moving like a crazy puppet's mouth, as if you were deaf. The doctor yanked on your penis with metal tongs, as if that would make it better.

Short, Sad Night

You tell me your first lover's breasts were perfect tight plums under your hands in her hot room. You used to leave before light with your school friends to hike in the mountains and eat a goat head along the way. You played accordion in a wedding band. In the army, you and Abdi used to lie down together on a bunk bed in the barracks and he'd read poetry into your hair:

> *A mountain begins with the first rock*
> *And man with the first pain.*

You tell me you shot at Iraqis flying over the swampy islands of Majnoon but the real battle was keeping the rats from your pillow at night. You told me that coming out of jail, you and Abdi took turns with an addicted girl no older than yourselves, who laid her hijab and raincoat carefully across a chair before lying down on the floor.

"What a short, sad night," you said.

You even told me how you planned to die, because you thought you'd changed your mind. You planned to turn on the gas oven in your apartment on Lansdowne, the oven in which we'd cooked pans of chicken kebob and kept the rice warm and made *chi*. You figured I'd ride up in the slow elevator and open your door and see your empty tea glass on the counter.

Under Number Eight

You told me many things. But you never told me what happened in jail. Abdi had to tell me about the room called Under Number Eight in the basement of the Mashad Military Headquarters. He told me that they opened your back with a cable as thick as your throat. That they bloodied your kidneys. That they covered your curly hair with a hood and beat at you until you looked like someone else. That they treated your wounds so they could start all over again.

I thought you'd told me everything. You even told me how you planned to kill yourself. How you'd turn on the gas. And I'd open the door and call out, "Jalal, I'm home."

You Gave Her Your Hand

There was always chicken kebob cooking in the oven and a pot of rice on the stove in your apartment on Lansdowne, and I'd take the elevator up, and it was slow, but I didn't mind.

Everyone would be there, and they'd be drinking tea or cooking opium and filling the air with poetry and someone would stand up and declare:

It's Night
Air standing like a hot, swollen body ...

Sometimes, the neighbour's pale kids would try to crawl over the balcony divide to get some food, and once their mother knocked on your door and said her name was Brenda and she wanted to join the party.

And Brenda sat on the floor with a plate of kebob and offered to read your palm. I laughed and said, "Come on, Jalal." But you actually gave her your hand.

And she put down her food and held your hand on her lap and traced the scars. And you stared over at her as if she had something you needed. You asked her how it would all turn out, and I just sat and watched.

Zap Valley

While I'm lying on a stretcher with yellow eyes and needle-pricked arms and a bedpan full of my strange brown pee and ugly white shit, you and Petra are getting all tangled up under the soft feather bed at her mother's apartment. I am sweating rancid stewed eggplant into the hospital sheets at the Frankfurt Krankenhaus F7 Isolation Ward and you are cheating on me. So hard and so long, that the neighbours shove a note under Petra's mother's apartment door: *Wenn you GIT IT OFF or ON, keep it PRIVAT!!!!*

Just last week, you and Petra were here at the hospital, standing down below my window like dedicated missionaries. It looked as though you were both worried sick about me and helping each other be brave. I was crouched by the half-open window, clutching my flimsy nightgown with one jaundiced hand and waving down at you with the hand hooked up to the IV. And Petra cried and waved back at me and then she walked away with you on those sturdy legs of hers.

Not to be rude, but Petra's the only big-thighed girl I know who would ever try to pull off a miniskirt. Fat ass, too.

Trumpener

When you phoned me on the Isolation Ward telephone, you were all sweet and silly. "Aren't they playing doctor with you all day long? That can't be all bad, can it? Getting your butt wiped by a man-nurse? I just might be jealous." I imagined you lying on an air mattress in Petra's brother's room, quietly slipping your hand down your pajama pants as you conjured up my red, swollen liver.

That night, my guts hurt so much, I crawled down the hospital halls looking for a nurse to comfort me. But that's the thing. Nobody in Isolation wants to touch you. Even if they wanted to, they're not allowed. The only man who comes near me now is the nursing aide who wrestles me out of bed and onto the wheelchair potty. In Ethiopia, he was a surgeon. Now his nimble hands are stuck on bedpan duty in a Krankenhaus ward full of infectious Germans and exceptions like me. We're both stuck in this ward of strict rules, special antiseptic soaps, and the endless sound of running water. If I want to play cards with Sonya in the next bed, I have to ask for latex gloves and so does she. "Hep Hep Hurray!" you cheer on the phone, just to make me laugh. "So bile your time and listen up: no games without a glove, is that what they're telling you?"

"He really used to love me," I tell Sonya. The Krankenschwester has turned off the lights for the night and locked us in, but Sonya can't sleep. I tell her you fell in love with me because I was the only girl at school with a postcard of the Al Aqsa Mosque in my locker. I tell her that you loved the fact that when you broke off part of your front tooth in some BBQ beef ribs at the Kim-Chi house in Calgary, I wanted to keep the shard. I tell her that you loved how I'd sneak out in the dark and sleep with you in the crappy shack behind your parents' house, a shack as narrow as a train roomette. "Keep it rocking and railing all night long," you used to say.

Your sister used to lock herself in the outhouse with a gym bag full of raw wieners and eat them until she puked. The night after a school play, her boyfriend tried to strangle her at a bush party near Terwilliger and she had to go to hospital. Her boyfriend had wild hair and he used to do Rockford turns on the ice in the driveway when he dropped her off at home. He'd speed up and then jerk the emergency brake really hard and they'd spin around and around and around. We could hear the spinning all the way out in our little shack. We sat out there and took acid once and believed our skin colour was changing for the better. We watched our flesh darken for hours, until we discovered that breath mints spark in the dark under blankets and we got busy with that instead.

I keep talking, until I hear Sonya start to snore very softly and then I just whisper. I tell her how you and I finally decided to escape the Prairies. That somewhere past Unity, Saskatchewan, some girls playing hackey sack tried to lure you off the Greyhound bus and into the hot, blowing wind. Through the bus window, we could see their blonde hair and laughing mouths and smooth knees. A herd of North Star running shoes were kicking up the dusty air around the bus stop. But you weren't fooled. You smiled and waved as we laughed and chewed our gum and called them Saskatchewan Sirens and Townie Tramps. You cuddled up against me and fell asleep. I watched white grain silos fall away into the dark.

You used to love to hear about my dreams, even when they

were complicated or kind of boring. Like the one where my family lived on the edge of the prairie in a cabin that didn't have a roof or a door or a floor. We slept on the grass and we were nervous all the time. We waited and waited for some kind of terrible attack, and finally we couldn't stand to wait anymore. We escaped at night across a river. And when we got to the other side, my family tried to fit in, even though we were from a different century. "That's it," I told you. "That's the end of my dream." You pretended to be deep in thought and then you said, "Well, I guess every country gets the foreigners it deserves." And you gave me a big kiss on the mouth.

When we went to stay in Israel, you loved that I was the only one on kibbutz brave enough to take Petra to the doctor in Kiryat Schmona. The sign outside said "Doctor Fröhlich. Skin and Venereal Diseases." His receptionist handed us a number – like at a butcher shop, number 79 – and told us to wait. Petra sighed and sat down and held her number until it was soggy with sweat and the number started to smudge. She wondered how long it would take to examine the inner kingdom of seventy-eight other girls.

I asked Petra if she blamed the really young guy who used to pedal over from Jericho on his bicycle and rub Dead Sea mud in her hair. Was it the Dutch man who kissed her in the tomato hot house in occupied Gaza? Or was it the soldier from Tabriz who worked in the kibbutz *reffet* cowshed and ordered her to scrape the manure stink off of him with her long nails? Petra thought he was probably the safest of the lot. He took Petra to visit his sister in Tel Aviv and play with her baby. He bought Petra Safari Pizza and kissed her in the damp sand near the sea wall. While they sat in the sand, he told Petra, "Your legs are like the sky, your legs are like the sky. So beautiful to look at!" It was all very romantic and he had these really intense eyes. But then, he was also the one who shot the cat dead on the kibbutz lawn. We would hit that cat's body every time we ran across to the bathrooms in the dark. It was the kind of thing that kept reminding us it was time to move on.

Petra said she preferred not to point fingers. But if she blamed anyone, it would probably be the girlfriend of the soccer player from Manaus who did that thing with unpeeled bananas. The doctor perched Petra in a weird gynecological chair and crouched down below her. He told her, "If the one doesn't want to, two don't argue." It was kind of like a scolding. Then we got back on the bus.

That was another thing you used to love about me. I could always figure out where the buses where going, even when the signs were written backwards.

And Petra came with us. In the end, when we finally figured out where to go and packed our bags and left the kibbutz for Turkey, she marched onto the ferry with her sturdy legs and a head scarf. We were bound for a village in the Zap Valley where hundreds of soldiers bounced guns in their laps and sipped hot tea.

In the middle of all those soldiers, their commander sucked a sugar cube and waved for us to join him in the tea garden. He smiled. He warned us the Zap Valley would not be what we imagined. He tried to sell us woolen socks his mother knit. You still have my pair in your suitcase.

We sat drinking sweet tea with the commander and his

Trumpener

soldiers while a bulldozer tore up the highway. You tossed your ball of knitted socks from hand to hand. Petra turned down extra sugar. I was anxious and mistook the village mad man for an old beggar woman. I kissed the beggar woman's dirty hand and pressed it to my forehead, out of respect. The commander laughed at my mistake and a soldier kicked the mad man in the leg. When it got late, the commander ordered us to hide inside our hotel. We walked down a path where a family stood behind barbed wire. They smiled and motioned for us to crawl under their fence. They fed us macaroni. They dressed me and Petra in bridal dresses from their mother and their grandmother. They offered me red lipstick. We stood there in white, Petra and I, arm in arm, smiling.

*

Now, you call the hospital to ask about my liver levels and my bilirubin numbers. You wonder if it's okay if you go away for a while. Petra's family has a cottage in Switzerland, where things are more neutral. You tell me you're itching to go. You say Petra's mother can keep an eye on me. I hold the phone for a long time. I study the sign taped to my hospital meal tray. It shows a pink pig covered with a big black X. All I can think is, "I'm eating fat free."

*

The day I first got sick, I started puking in a toilet stall already flooded ankle-deep with water. You sloshed in there to get me out. For days, you urged me to try tiny sips of water and dry bread crumbs and spoonfuls of yogurt. "Just a tiny taste, oh Typhoid Mary, just a wee last supper." You sent Petra out for a doctor or drugs. You sang me Simon and Garfunkel songs and promised I would be okay. All night long, a woman wept loudly in the room next door. She cried, "Allah, Allah, Allahhhhh!"

You and Petra plotted how you'd get me and my yellow skin and yellow eyes out of bed, across the border, and through Customs and Immigration. In the end, Petra covered me up with her head scarf and a long raincoat. She helped you to walk me onto a plane bound for her hometown. I slumped in the seat between you and Petra, bitter about my liver. You held my hand until I fell asleep.

THANKS for THAWING my FROZEN TONGUE to:

MY CANDLEFISH CREATIVE CLAN:
Al Rempel, Laisha Rosnau, Gillian Wigmore

THE INSPIRATIONS:
Michelle Blair, Gord Thompson, Jenny Brundin, Beata
Polanska, Katie & Mom.

WRITERS I COSIED UP WITH IN THE BURNING COLD:
Lynda Williams, Michelle Read, Hilary Crowley, Sheila Peters
& Creekstone Press, the late Trish Janz, George Sipos, Donna
Kane, Harold Rhenisch, Jacqui Baldwin, Frances Rose, my radio
roommates.

THE TORONTO WOMEN WRITERS:
Sheila Stewart—from Improv to Genesis, Liz Ukrainetz,
Maureen Hynes, Elisse Levine's wild rides.

THE FAIRY GODPARENTS:
Susie Wheeler, Andy Schlitt, Tanja Gattrell, Amanda Batho.

MY FOREVERS:
Charlie & Daisy, Dad & John, Nadya, Lynne, Loren, Christine,
Sarah, Lisa, Melanie, Indra, Randall, Karen, Jane, Lisa, Mary
Lou, Leela, Heather, Louise, Kibbutz Cathy, Gilat, Giulliana.

THIS POWERFUL & PRETTY PUBLISHING POSSE:
Vici Johnstone, Patricia Wolfe, Meg Taylor, Marissa Alps.

EARLY BELIEVERS in ARTS ACHIEVERS:
The Toronto Arts Council, the Ontario Arts Council, the
Emma Lake Writers/Artists Colony in Saskatchewan, the BC
Festival of the Arts.

Acknowledgements

Earlier versions of some of these stories appeared in *The Malahat Review, Event, Queen Street Quarterly, SubTerrain, dig, Monday Magazine, Reflections on Water, Northword Magazine, Letting Go* [Black Moss Press, 2005], *The Fed Anthology* [Anvil Press, 2003], *Outskirts* [Sumach Press, 2002], and *Exact Fare Only* [Anvil Press, 2000], or were broadcast on CBC Radio's *North by Northwest*.

More fiction and poetry from Caitlin Press

A Well-Mannered Storm: The Glenn Gould Poems, Kate Braid, 120 pp, pb, ISBN: 978-1-894759-28-1, $16.95

Lan(d)guage: A Sequence of Poetics, Ken Belford, 88 pp, pb, ISBN: 978-1-894759-29-X, $16.95

Pathways into the Mountains, Ken Belford, poetry, 94 pp, pb ISBN: 978-0-920576-84-7, $14.95

Soft Geography, Gillian Wigmore, poetry, 80 pp, pb, ISBN: 978-1-894759-23-6, $15.95

All Things Said & Done, Marita Dachsel, poetry, 80 pp, pb, ISBN: 978-1-894759-22-9, $15.95

Finding Ft. George, Rob Budde, poetry, 128 pp, pb, ISBN: 978-1-894759-27-4, $15.95

A Northern Woman, Jaqueline Baldwin, poetry, 150 pp, pb ISBN: 978-1-894759-01-4, $16.95

The Last Three Hundred Miles, G. Stewart Nash, fiction, 168 pp, pb, ISBN: 978-0-920576-90-8, $18.95